D0095128

WORLD SONG

Also by Ann Nolan Clark

IN MY MOTHER'S HOUSE

LITTLE NAVAJO BLUEBIRD

SECRET OF THE ANDES

LOOKING-FOR-SOMETHING

BLUE CANYON HORSE

SANTIAGO

THIRD MONKEY

A SANTO FOR PASQUALITA

WORLD SONG

BY ANN NOLAN CLARK

ILLUSTRATED BY KURT WIESE

WITHDRAWN

THE VIKING PRESS · NEW YORK

DELTA COLLEGE LIBRARY

CHILD LITERATURE COLLECTION

Copyright © 1960 by Ann Nolan Clark
First published in 1960 by The Viking Press, Inc.
625 Madison Avenue, New York 22, N.Y.
Published in Canada by The Macmillan Company of Canada Limited

Child. Lit. PZ 7 .C5296 Wo 1

Clark, Ann Nolan, 1898-

World song

PRINTED IN THE U.S.A. BY THE VAIL-BALLOU PRESS, INC.

To my grandson

Patrick Nolan Clark

WORLD SONG

Chapter One

The plane, a silver-winged bird, flew high above the earth against a gray-cloud-blanket sky. It cut through time and distance, on and on, hour after hour, mile after mile.

The passengers read and slept and talked—all but one, a redheaded boy. He did not read, or sleep, or talk.

Patrick Joseph Barrington the Third—but known to everyone, even his mother, as Red—pressed his freckled nose against the plane window. He sat still, almost breathlessly still, looking down at the world below. The other passengers looked at him and smiled. Such an alert, clean-looking boy, they thought. He looked alive and restless even though he sat so still. They wondered why he was alone. They wondered where he had come from and where he was going.

Red did not know their thoughts. He scarcely knew that they were there. He sat sideways in the seat, his thin, young shoulders hunched forward under the new plaid shirt, his bright head leaning against the windowpane. A few who caught a glimpse of the freckled face beneath the red hair thought, What a happy boy! Then a second thought quickly followed: But something troubles him. They wondered what it was.

Something was troubling the boy—a small but sharp, insistent trouble in the midst of his happiness. For Red was happy. He felt almost bursting with happiness. He was happy about the plane ride, about his being allowed to travel alone. He was happy about the visit with Gramp at the end of the flight. After that visit there would be the Great Adventure, so close now, only a month or two away. But the troubled feeling was sharp. What would Gramp think about his going? Would he be terribly lonely?

The pretty stewardess stopped beside his seat. She wanted to talk with him, but the boy did not know that she was there. It was as if there were no others on the plane. He was alone with earth and sky, flying as a bird would fly.

He had boarded the plane in Chicago, in the dark hour just before the dawn. He had come down the aisle in an eager rush, bringing a breath of stinging cold with him, waving back and calling in an excited whisper, "I'll be all right. Don't worry. I'll be fine." Then the roar of whirling propellers had cut off sound. The plane taxied down the runway, turned, waiting, gathering power, then with a mighty run and lift soared smoothly into the night sky. The lights of the airport dimmed in size, in importance, in reality.

At first Red had been a little afraid, but soon fear passed into the joy of flight. This was his first trip on a plane, his first alone. He had come west before, many times. But always before he had come by train or car and always with some member of his family. So, in a way, this was his first trip. In a way it was his last trip, too. At least it would be the last he would make to the western country for a long time. At the thought, the small cloud passed across his face again, chasing the happy look away for the moment. He worried. Will Gramp think I should stay with him? Maybe I shouldn't go. But he knew he would go. He wanted to go. It would be the most exciting, the most wonderful thing. But Gramp would be left behind.

Red's parents knew about his worry. They knew his joy was lessened by his concern for his grandfather. They knew that his grandfather would miss him. The two were so alike. They were so companionable and so close. They worried, too, about the old one who would be left alone. So they gave their son this extra time for a last visit before he went on what he called his Great Adventure.

Inside the plane, Red pressed his face against the window glass. The lights of Chicago were twinkling and dancing like an army of fireflies in a fairyland of light. Every house was lighted and every room, or so it seemed. Red wondered if the people who lived down there ever slept, ever turned the lights off and went to bed in quiet darkness.

He thought that the giant plane must seem very small between the emptiness of the sky and the crowded bigness of the land. Its lights blinked red and green, red and green. As the boy watched their blinking he forgot his worry. Once again he was filled at the wonder of what lay before him.

Perhaps he dozed awhile. He did not mean to waste a

single second by sleeping it away. But when he looked again the sun had risen. Clear and warm and bright it shone down on the fenced fields, the tidy farm houses, and the straight roadways of the Middle West.

Breakfast was served. Red was hungry. Not missing a bite, he managed somehow to keep his gaze turned downward on the world beneath the speeding plane.

Now they were flying low over tiny, toy-sized towns crisscrossed with streets that were filled with hurrying people walking on them. They flew over paved highways where cars and buses and trucks hustled along like lines of insects marching. Once, circling a landing field, they flew over a town square where midget men on matchstick ladders were hanging some kind of banners for a town celebration.

The plane flew high and low and banked and sometimes circled. Sometimes it landed at airports where passengers got off and others got on. Then it taxied and stopped and roared again and rose upward smoothly into the sky. Airports and people and houses and trees became little and unimportant and unreal.

Towns and farm houses were farther apart now. The flat land became rougher, broken, and at last untended and unplanted. Then there were hills. Then rounded mountains. The plane climbed upward to fly over their tree-covered tops.

The mountain air was rough. There were flurries of snow. The smooth flight became uneven. The plane bounced and dipped, hitting air pockets, losing altitude, then righting itself again. The stewardess brought lunch and placed the tray carefully on a pillow in the boy's lap. Red looked around at the other passengers. It was the first time he had noticed anything except the world outside. He smiled at the fat man across the aisle and at the man's coffee, which was jumping up and down in its cup. "Choppy, isn't it?" Red said, pleased that he knew the right word. The man nodded, putting the coffee cup back on the tray.

The woman beside him leaned across to speak to the boy. "How old are you?" she asked, pleasant but curious.

"Going on thirteen. I was twelve last week," Red told her, spooning the last bite of ice cream from its plastic carton.

"Are you traveling alone?" the woman asked.

"Yes'm," Red answered, turning again to the window. Silly question, he thought. Couldn't she see he was traveling alone?

The world below the great plane's wings was very different now. The earth was red. It was torn and gashed by deep arroyos. Stunted trees grew in clumps, tired-looking, old-looking, twisted and bent. Gray bushes leaned against the wind. Cactus clumps stood solid and stiff, half buried in hills of sand. Neither storm nor wind could sway them or turn them or bend them. They stood solid and still.

Far off a brown ribbon of river cut through the cornfields and wound around clusters of flat-topped shoebox houses of earth-colored adobe. "Indian country," Red whispered excitedly. Although his home was in the Middle West and this was just vacation land, when he was away from it he was always lonely for this sandy, barren land. He wished he could live here always and never leave it. It was his country —his and the Indians who lived here.

The plane banked, climbing swiftly. Snow-capped peaks of the Sangre de Cristo mountains came rushing close. The plane climbed higher, higher. Gray clouds enfolded it. Moving, furling masses of soft gray pushed against the window glass. The plane cut through them cleanly. Then the clouds parted, and the sun shone down on jagged, rocky peaks, ice-draped in freezing blue.

Now the plane was over the Jemez range. One peak stood proudly alone, topping all others in height and majesty. It was Mount Taylor, Sacred Mountain of the Navajo, and one of the corners of the Navajo world. "Mother of the Rain," Red said—its Navajo name.

He flattened his nose against the window glass. He could not get enough of looking. He strained his eyes to see this shrine, this holy place of the Navajo Indians which held their magic and their power. All he could see were sheer rock walls and ice and snow and deep, woundlike, purple gorges. Mount Taylor, Mother of the Rain, guarded its secret world.

The stewardess sat down beside him. "Patrick," she said. "You are Patrick, aren't you?"

The boy dragged his gaze from the wild world outside the plane. "Yes'm," he answered politely.

"Is this your first plane trip?"

"Yes'm," he answered again. He wished she would go away. He wished she would not bother him with questions —not now, when they were almost over the Navajo Reservation.

"You came from Chicago, didn't you?" The stewardess was determined to be friendly with this friendly-looking boy who would not talk. "Is Chicago your home?"

Reluctantly the boy turned from the window. This question-and-answer game was going to take time. He might as well get on with it. "I live in Middlebury, north of Chicago."

"How nice to live in Middlebury."

The boy nodded, but did not answer.

A small silence began to settle comfortably between them. But the stewardess would not have it so. Cheerfully she asked another question. "What does your father do in Middlebury?"

Red sighed. This was the way grown-ups were. Perhaps they could not help it. Perhaps it was part of being grown-up. "My father teaches at Middlebury College," he told her, stealing a glance at the world outside.

"You are going to Gallup, aren't you? That's our next stop."

"Yes'm," Red answered.

"Are you visiting in Gallup?"

Would she never stop talking? Would she never go away? "About a hundred miles from Gallup. At a trading post. My grandfather is a trader to the Navajos."

This time he turned his back. He looked out the window. "Look!" he cried excitedly. "There are the red rocks. We're over the Reservation now, or anyway almost. Look at those red rocks. Aren't they high and red and bare and beautiful!"

Far below on a wind-swept plain the red rocks of the Navajo Reservation thrust upward a thousand feet from the dry sand wastes.

At the front of the plane the red light flashed on the sign, FASTEN SEAT BELTS. The stewardess walked down the aisle to see that belts were fastened. The plane banked and dropped, dropped and circled.

The town of Gallup sprawled out among the sand dunes, a tangle of streets, a huddle of houses, a handful of white people in a pocket of an Indian world.

Red's heart thumped. His fingers were clammy as he wiggled into his sweater and topcoat. Any minute now he would see his grandfather. Soon he would see Hasteen, his

Indian best friend. He would see Hasteen's father, who was called Yellow-Shirt's-Son. He would see Hasteen's grandfather, who was Yellow-Shirt, a powerful Navajo medicine man. He would see Shemah, Hasteen's mother, who was housekeeper for Gramp at the Trading Post. He would see all the other Indians whom he knew and liked.

Soon, soon, soon he would be at home again in this land that he loved and longed for when he was away from it.

Suddenly, in the midst of his excitement, the sad thought came back to him, like a cold wind blowing the clouds across the face of the sun. This would be his last visit for two years, two long, long years. There would be no more long, lazy summer vacations or short, happy Christmas holidays. Two years! His mother said that two years would pass quickly. His father said two years were nothing measured in a lifetime. But what would Gramp say? I'll ask him. He'll tell me, the boy promised himself.

The plane thumped gently, landing, and taxied smoothly to the airport gate. The travelers walked stiffly down the tipped-up aisle. They stepped gingerly out on the steps. Then they were on pavement. Their feet were on solid, good earth once more.

Red had no time for thinking. There was no room for sad thoughts in the fullness of his happiness. He was home. He always called it home, although his family teased him about it. He said Middlebury was where he lived, but the Navajo country was home. He tucked his overnight case more firmly under his arm. He clutched his muffler, mittens, cap, and overshoes and walked with the other passengers across the pavement and through the gate.

His grandfather was there, waiting for him, welcoming

him with outstretched hand. One of the best things about
Gramp, Red thought, was that he did not hug you as if you
were a baby. He shook your hand, man-to-man.

"You made it, Red."

"I made it, Gramp."

Young hand tucked into the old hand's pocket, a tousled,
redheaded boy and a shaggy, white-haired man walked into
the airport building. How alike they were. It was easy to
know that they both were Patrick Joseph Barrington. That
one was the First and one was the Third made only the years
between them different.

They went to get the suitcases and to send a telegram back
to a waiting mother. They spoke to everyone. Everyone
knew them.

"He made it," Gramp told them.

"I'm here," Red added.

Outside an April sun brightened the afternoon. A wind
teased the last snow patches, nibbling their edges.

Red was impatient. "If we get started, Gramp, we can
eat up those miles and get to the Trading Post almost before
the sun goes down."

His grandfather laughed. It was good to have the boy
here. He wished they would leave him here for the next
two years. But they would not. He had argued with them.
Letters had flown back and forth between Middlebury and
the Trading Post—letters that Red did not know about. The
boy's parents would not be persuaded by argument. Their
minds were made up. Red must go with them. "Red should
go with them," the old man argued with himself. "It's the
chance of a lifetime for the young fellow. If I were younger,
I'd go along with him."

"Let's go, Gramp." Red tugged at his grandfather's sleeve. "If we don't get going, we'll never get there."

The old man laughed again. "I was woolgathering," he said.

They went out to the parking area where grandfather had left his car.

Chapter Two

The car skimmed over the black-top highway, away from Gallup, away from town. Snow melted and ran in trickles of yellow water into the ever-thirsty sandbanks at the sides of the road. The air had the fresh, clean smell of newly-washed piñon and cedar. It was clear and sparkling, sun-warmed, with only a hint of springtime wind around the edges of the afternoon.

At first Red had neither thoughts nor words—just happiness at coming home. He saw a hogan in the distance, blue smoke curling up from its center smokehole. "They say at

school that hogans look like beehives," he told his grandfather.

"Well, they do," Gramp said, chuckling.

A small Navajo girl ran across the road. Her long, wide
skirt petaled flower-like around her tiny, moccasined feet.
Silver bells tied to her sash fringe and moccasin buttons
made a tinkle of sound sharp and clear above the noise of
the motor. The sheep that she was herding stared stupidly
at the slowing car. Quail, like church-going ladies in new
Sunday hats, hurried along bowing and nodding. A road-
runner, racing the car, braked its speed with its long tail.
It looked around amazed and amused as if saying, "Whew!
I didn't know how fast I was going."

Red laughed. He had forgotten all the little things he loved
about this country. When he was away all he could think of
was that he missed it and wanted to come back again. Now
he strung all the little things together, the smells, the sights,
the sounds that made the chain that held him here.

Turning from the car window, he looked up at his grandfather. "I thought Hasteen would come with you to meet
me," he said. "Why didn't he come? Is he still in school?"

"Hasteen?" Gramp asked.

Aha, Red thought. Woolgathering again. "Yes, Hasteen.
Why didn't he come to meet me?"

"He is in school," Gramp said. "When he gets here he
will have news for you. They are sending him to the Albuquerque Indian School this summer. He will be leaving
soon, I think."

Red was excited. "He will? Why Albuquerque? Does he
want to go?"

Grandfather chuckled. The conversation was taking the
turn he had hoped it would. "Does he want to go? Of course

he wants to go. Anyone"—Grandfather's voice became very hearty—"anyone who has an opportunity to go new places is happy about it."

Red looked at his grandfather. He thought, I won't need to ask him. He is trying to tell me. Suddenly he knew his going would be all right. He and his grandfather were going to talk about it, and everything would be fine.

He grinned at his grandfather. "Looks like snow, doesn't it Gramp?" he said conversationally.

Secretly his grandfather was pleased. He's a smart one, he thought; can't fool that boy. Aloud he said, "All right, young fellow, let's face it. Seems like Hasteen isn't the only boy who is going places. Heard that you were going with your mother and dad to Central America. Sounds like a mighty fine trip to me."

Red was silent. His blue eyes looked straight ahead. His heart thumped. Shall I ask him straight out? he thought. Shall I say I won't go, Gramp, if you don't want me to go?

His grandfather spoke. His voice was serious and more than a little firm. "Tell me about it," he said. Red knew that voice. It meant, Tell me. Tell me the truth. Tell me everything.

He answered slowly. "Dad had a chance to go to Costa Rica to experiment with cacao growing. Cacao," he explained, "is what they call chocolate in Costa Rica." Red was quiet for a while, but grandfather was even more quiet. After a little the silence became uncomfortable, so Red talked again. He said, "Dad says it's his big chance. One he has always wanted. Dad will leave next week, and then he will send for Mom and—" Red stopped talking, to catch his breath, to turn his face away. Then he added, "They say I'm going, too."

Grandfather guided the car skillfully along the road. "Do you want to go?" he asked quietly.

"Yes," Red answered softly. "Yes, I want to go, but I don't want to leave you. What will you do without me? It's for two years—two years!"

The old man sighed. To him, now that he was getting old, the years came rushing by with frightful swiftness. To the boy, being young, they were unending. He supposed that only to his son, Red's father, were two years of rightful length. But how could he explain this to the boy beside him, to the boy who thought two years were a lifetime? He wished the boy could stay with him, but not for anything would he say this. The boy must go. It would be a good thing for him to see new lands, new people, new ways of living. It must not be spoiled with worry about an old man who would miss him.

Grandfather was lonely now that his children had grown and had left the Reservation for faraway cities. Red was his only grandson, and the pride of his life. Time for him between the Christmas holidays and summer vacations was just a waiting time for the boy to come again. But he must not let an old man's needs be as rocks in a new, untraveled trail. But how to tell the young boy this?

Finally he spoke. "Well, I'll miss you, Red, and you'll miss me. That's a fact. We would not want to change it. But walking right up to a fact and facing it often puts it right where it belongs. Let's make this fact walk behind us. We know it's there, but it stays behind. It does not go along in front of us, bumping into the new things we want to see along the way. We'll miss each other, but you must go. Way the world is today, you'd best get to know all kinds of different people and how to get along with them."

"Oh, I can get along with people all right," Red said. "I get along with the boys at school and the Indians here on the Reservation."

Grandfather looked doubtful. "Yes, but here in your own country you have things in common with the people around you. You have things you share together without thinking much about it."

Red nodded, but he only half heard what his grandfather was saying. His thoughts were about facing facts and putting them where they belonged. He felt better about leaving his grandfather. They'd miss each other, but his grandfather wanted him to go. That helped.

Grandfather was still talking. "The Navajos say every man walks his trail alone. When trails cross, that's fine and good. But we must learn to walk our trail alone."

Companionable silence filled the car as it lurched over the frozen, rutty road. Along the sides were hills of crepe-paper sand that had been fluted by the wind's restless fingers. Overhead an unseen jet unraveled its threadlike trail across the sky.

Red leaned forward to look. It could not be. It was! There against the towering red rocks and the flaming sunset sky was the Trading Post. There was the water hole, red now with the sky's reflected color. There was Desbah, taking her sheep to the night corral behind her mother's hogan.

Saddled horses stood, heads lowered, reins trailing the ground, in front of the long, low stone building that was the Trading Post. Red knew the horses as he knew their riders. The sorrel belonged to Song-Singer. The tired old mare was Gray-Eye's favorite. That neat black one over there was a racer. It belonged to Fred Begay, the Day School teacher.

The car bumped to a stop before the long, gray building.

Yellow-Shirt's-Son came out to greet them, to put the car away.

"When will Hasteen get here?" Red asked him.

"Maybe next week, maybe tomorrow," the Navajo answered. Time meant little to him. Hasteen would come, but when was not important.

Inside, the Trading Post was as it had been always, as Red remembered it. On one side from floor to ceiling were the shelves of canned goods, their labels bright and tempting. On the other side from floor to ceiling were the shelves of dry goods, bolts of many colors of velvet, sateen, and Indian calico. From the ceiling rafters—*vigas* the Indians called them—hung bridles with silver disks, carved, silver-trimmed saddles, and clinking silver spurs. From the vigas also hung coils of rope and hand-woven saddle blankets.

Hardware was kept under the counters—tin pails, enamel kettles, axes and shovels, hammers and saws and coffee pots. It seemed to be a hopeless collection of things, but Gramp knew without looking where to put his hand on everything.

In the glass cases were cheap watches and alarm clocks, pink toilet soap, ladies' sidecombs set with colored glass beads, and cards and cards of safety pins. Nothing was changed. Everything was in the place it had been always. Everything was as it should be.

At the back of the long room a corner was partitioned. This was the post office. Red remembered, when he was very young, reading the sign, UNITED STATES POST OFFICE, and thinking this must be the most important place in all the world.

At each side of the store was a door leading into small rooms. In one of these rooms pawn was kept. Red looked to see if a certain concho belt was still there. It had been there last year. Gray-Eyes had pawned it. It was gone now. Wool prices must have been good, Red thought, so Gray-Eyes could redeem his belt. Almost all of the pawn pieces were gone. The room was filled with new belts and necklaces, rings and buttons of silver and coral, shell, turquoise and obsidian. There were a few old pieces, many old designs and some that were new. The new designs were very good, quite modern, but also quite Indian. Tomorrow, the boy decided, he would spend the day asking Yellow-Shirt's-Son about each piece. The Navajo man would want to tell him. No matter what he had planned for the day, it could be postponed. The time would be well spent in telling the Old One's grandson things that he should know. Navajos believed that children were important, and time spent with them was time well spent.

Red looked around the store again. Nothing was changed. The other small room opposite the silver room was the blanket room where thousands of pounds of Navajo blankets were waiting shipment to the nearby wholesale houses in Gallup. Red looked in the room and sniffed the thick sheep smell of wool. He liked it. It was a coming-home smell. He picked up a saddle blanket, wondering if he could still estimate its weight correctly. Suddenly he grinned, remembering his teacher at Middlebury who would not believe that Navajos sell their blankets by pound rather than size.

Yellow-Shirt's-Son came in from putting the car away. He said, in Navajo, "You buzz around like a mosquito. You can't see everything tonight. Wait until tomorrow."

Red laughed and the Navajos lounging around the red-hot stove in the center of the store laughed also. They laughed in the Navajo way, not by sound, but a silent wave of laughter that broke against the quietness of time. Red did not see them laugh or hear them, but he felt their laughter. He knew they were pleased that he was here again. They were pleased that he had been spoken to in Navajo and that he had understood. Deep Indian pleasure settled comfortably around the stove.

Gramp came into the store. He said to his grandson, "Shemah has supper ready. She wants us to come."

They went through the back storerooms where cane sugar and wheat flour and Irish potatoes were kept in hundred-pound sacks, where coffee and lard and syrup were kept in giant tin containers, where sheep hides were stacked against the wall and wool in bales was piled for shipping. They went through a heavy, iron-barred door, across a narrow hall, and through a second door. Then they were in another world. Here was a long, white-walled, white-washed room. The walls were covered with Navajo blankets and wild-animal skins. Hanging from the vigas of the low ceiling were Indian baskets from the basket-weaving tribes. On the worn, wide-planked floor were more rugs, more animal skins. In the wide-silled windows were pots of geraniums, bows and arrows, clay pots, stone fetishes, ancient bone knives. A great stone fireplace was at the end of the room, and now it was filled with glowing, crackling, sweet-smelling cedar logs. Tables, stools, and chairs were made of hand-carved, sturdy pine and covered with cowhide. It was an attractive room, bright and friendly and much lived in.

Shemah was waiting for Gramp and Red to come to the evening meal. Shemah was Yellow-Shirt's-Son's wife and Hasteen's mother. Since Grandmother died Shemah had been Gramp's housekeeper. Red loved her, he thought, almost as much as he loved Mom—not quite as much, perhaps, but almost as much. Now he went to greet her, to touch her finger tips briefly in the most delicate of handshakes. This was the Navajo way.

"Do I still have the little room for my museum?" he asked her. This also was the Navajo way—not to say, "How are you?" or "I'm glad I'm here," but to take up conversation again as if he had not been away. Besides, he wanted to know if the little room was still his room for the treasures he had collected. The little room had been his grandmother's sewing room, and for a long time it was as she had left it. Then last year Gramp had surprised him by fixing it over for a place for Red to keep his treasures.

"Is it still my room?" Red repeated.

Shemah nodded, but spoke quickly, softly. "Not to go there now. Now is to wash and to eat the food."

The others were eating when Red came back, his red hair plastered wetly to his head, every freckle shining from a soap-and-water scrubbing. Besides Gramp there were four other men at the table. That was the way it always was at the Trading Post. Red could not remember ever having eaten a meal with just the family present. On the Reservation, where distances were great and towns were few, Gramp's Trading Post was known far and wide as a wayside stopping place. All kinds of people stopped there for a meal or a night, or a week if need be. Gramp's hospitality was casual but unfailing.

Tonight there were Yellow-Shirt's-Son and the Day School teacher on his way to Gallup, a traveling government-service dentist, and a prospector for uranium.

Shemah piled their plates with stewed mutton, Mexican beans, and fried bread. There were bowls of cold canned tomatoes and dried apricots on the table to be passed around "family style," as Gramp said. Shemah did not eat with the men, but stood beside Gramp, replenishing the plates quietly.

Red said little. He was too hungry. But while he ate he listened to the talk. Yellow-Shirt, the old medicine man, had gone to the mountains to gather holy plants for the Fire Dance which was to be held in a few days. The teacher told about the trailer schools which were being opened in the areas of the reservation where there were no roads and no permanent settlements. Dotted over the Reservation were many deep wells which the government had drilled to supply water to Indians and their flocks of sheep and horse herds. Near these wells trailers were to be hauled in and set up as schoolrooms for Navajo children who came with their parents for water. It was another way to get the children into school. Perhaps, having water and a school nearby, the nomads would build hogans and settle down for at least a part of every year. The teacher said that if they did this the government would build a permanent school where the trailers had been.

Schools! Red thought. He wondered if there was a place left anywhere that was so far from a school a boy would not have to go.

The traveling dentist made his rounds also by trailer. He took his tools with him as he traveled the Indian back-country. He went to the end of the roads and camped there. The Indians came to him, on horseback and in wagons over the sand-filled trails.

The prospector did not talk. Like Red, he seemed too hungry to waste time in conversation. Looking at him, Red decided that he was even too hungry to listen to the others talking. Gramp motioned to Shemah to fill the prospector's plate again.

After supper the men sat in front of the fire in the big stone fireplace. They were still talking, exchanging the news of the back places, of the trail, and of the world outside the Reservation. The prospector slept, snoring gently. Red slipped away.

He went into the little room that was now his museum. It was as he had left it. All his treasures were in place and all were neatly labeled in his best school printing. On this shelf were his birds' nests, the old, abandoned ones he and Hasteen had found on their exploring trips. Red touched each one with gentle fingers. This one was a warbler's nest made of willow stems and leaves and grass. He had found it last year after the birds had left it. Maybe this year, since he had come so early, he might see the birds nesting, even hatching. Red liked birds, all kinds, but the tiny warblers were his favorites.

When Hasteen comes I must tell him what a beautiful song the warbler has and how he flies in the air singing his heart out as he flies higher and higher, Red thought; that man who visited school knew a lot about birds. He wished he could sing the warbler's song. He tried to whistle it and then to hum it, but he could not. He could hear it, but he could not imitate its sound.

He walked along looking at all his treasures, one by one. This ball of moss with the tiny doorway in one side belonged to the water ouzel. Once, when he and Hasteen had gone with Yellow-Shirt to the mountains for holy plants, they had found this nest on a rock ledge by a stream. Slowly he walked along, fingering the long, hanging nest of the oriole, the piece of hollow tree trunk that once had belonged to a woodpecker and later to a desert sparrow-hawk.

He stopped before the old Singer sewing machine that

had been his grandmother's. He remembered very little about his grandmother—only that she had been small and gay and always wore a white apron with lace on it and peppermint candy in its pocket.

On top of the sewing machine he kept his collection of birds' eggs in box tops lined with cotton. Now he looked at them, turquoise, cream, spotted, brown, all colors, all sizes and many shapes. He remembered his latest possession. Just before he left last year he had traded an agate, two glassies, and an old baseball mitt to the government doctor's son for two pale-green eggs with brown freckles. He thought they belonged to a nuthatch. Suddenly he remembered that he had brought a bird book with him. It was in his suitcase in the room Gramp called Red's Room across the hall.

He went across the hall, opened the door, turned on the light, and stopped in amazement. Covering the walls were neatly framed water-color pictures of birds. He went closer. Hasteen had painted them as a surprise for him.

Near the door was a picture of a yellow warbler—black cap, yellow breast, green back, almost flitting through a background of willow leaves. Next to it was a golden eagle in a yellow pine, a mourning dove, a jewel-like humming bird. They were there, all the ones he knew—a bluebird, a meadow lark, a woodpecker—and each one told a story. He looked at the picture of the camp robber, remembering the time he and Hasteen were camping in Blue Canyon and a camp robber came right on their rock table and stole their tortillas. The quail picture made him remember their pack trip to Oasis Ranch and the quail walking in a sedate line to the pool for their morning drink. Next was a picture of two swallows sipping raindrops as they flew—making him remember a rainstorm long ago on a summer day.

Each feather, each jaunty cap, each graceful wing tip had been captured by the brush strokes of his Indian friend. It must have taken many hours to remember backward and to catch in a picture each happy day he and Red had spent together.

Red's breath caught in his throat. This was Hasteen's way of saying good-by. When will our trails cross again? he wondered. When I have gone to Costa Rica? What will Costa Rica be like? He had read all the books in the school library about this small country of Central America. But what would it really be like when he was there? Would he find a friend like Hasteen?

The boy undressed, turned off the light, and got into the bed that always was waiting for him when he returned.

By and by the door opened softly. Gramp came in carrying a lighted kerosene lamp. The Trading Post had electric lights, but Gramp never trusted them. A lamp was different —Gramp trusted a lamp. It always gave a light if it was filled with kerosene, and Shemah saw to it that it was always full. Gramp put the light on the table and sat on the edge of his grandson's bed. "Good pictures, don't you think?" he asked, nodding toward the pictures on the wall. "Hasteen has talent. He should be an artist, but he wants to be a mechanic. That's what he's going to be, he says, starting his training when he goes to Albuquerque."

Red sat up in bed. "I wish he was coming with me. I wish you were coming, Gramp. Wouldn't it be something special if we three could see Costa Rica together?"

"Sometimes trails cross when one least expects them to," Gramp said. "Like now, for instance. Hasteen is here. Caught a ride in a truck. Couldn't wait for the bus in the morning."

"Hasteen? Where?" Red cried, jumping out of bed.

"Here." Gramp chuckled, pushing the door open for the Indian boy to enter.

Hasteen was taller than he had been at Christmas time, taller and thinner. Black hair, black eyes, bronze skin, and flashing smile—Hasteen looked as Red remembered him. He was the same. He had not changed. He is still my friend, Red thought; my Indian best friend.

Small, silent seconds held the boys apart. Then their shyness broke, and words flowed like flood waters over a dam. Most of the conversation was in English, but when English was not enough, Hasteen spoke in Navajo. Red understood. He did not speak the Indian language; he could not master the sounds. But he understood it.

"Chattering magpies," Gramp grumbled. But he was pleased. He was very fond of the young Indian boy. As for Red, when Gramp thought of how much he loved the redhead, mist stung his eyes and pain numbed his tongue. So he spoke gruffly. "Chattering magpies."

After the first bit of catching up, the boys were silent. They had lots of time. They would be together six whole days.

Shemah came to the door. "Telephone," she told Gramp. "Food," she said to Hasteen. She looked at the redheaded boy. "Sleep," she said softly, herding the other two out of the room.

The bedroom door closed, and after a while the Trading Post slept under a Navajo moon.

Chapter Three

"Only one more day!" Red said sadly, "Boy! Have we been busy. Horseback trip to Rainbow Bridge. Camping overnight with Gramp. Helping at sheep dip. It's been the best vacation we've had."

Hasteen agreed. "Yes, it's been a good vacation, but vacations can't last forever. Monday I begin a new way."

Red looked thoughtfully at his friend. Navajos were like that, he thought. Their tribe could take on new ways quickly and with enjoyment. They could take on an entirely new way of life and still remain Navajos. Aloud he asked, although he knew the answer, "Do you want to go to the Albuquerque school? Everything will be different from school here on the Reservation."

Hasteen nodded. "Yes, I know that, but I will like it, I think. I want to be a mechanic. They say I can learn that there."

"Gramp says you should be an artist. He says you have talent."

Again the Indian boy nodded. "I love to paint. When I am painting, nothing else matters. But I want to be a mechanic." He hesitated. Then he said slowly, "I'm Indian, so I must live in two worlds. My Indian world is my painting world." He looked at Red and smiled. "Working with machinery is the work of my White world. You, my friend, belong to that world."

Red was displeased. He did not want Hasteen to have a private world where he could not enter. He did not want his Indian friend to be different in any way. He said quickly, "You and I are alike."

The Indian boy smiled again. He spoke softly. "No one is like anyone else, not really, but we have many things that we share. Maybe the things we share make us feel alike. I do not know. We could ask my grandfather, Yellow-Shirt. He is very wise. He knows such things."

The younger boy was not convinced. "We don't look alike or maybe act alike, but deep inside we must be alike. Why else would we be such good friends?"

"We are friends because of the things we share." The Indian boy was stubborn. He had a calm, quiet stubbornness without anger or irritation.

Shemah came into the room. Although Shemah was Hasteen's mother, Red had always had her love, her gentle service. They had been his as much as Hasteen's. Red looked at the Navajo woman with a new awareness. He saw an Indian woman, middle-aged, tall, thin, strong-looking, and graceful. Her hair was black as night. She wore it combed back from her forehead, clubbed at her neck, and bound with homespun yarn. Her eyes were wide-set, keen, and very dark. Her cheek bones were high, and her smile flashed whitely across her bronze-skinned face, as Hasteen's did. Red looked at her velvet blouse, her wide calico skirts, the tips of her small brown moccasins. He smiled across at Hasteen. Yes, he thought, he and Hasteen shared many things. Shemah was one of them.

"Coffee? Fried bread?" Shemah asked, putting a slender finger against her lips. Both boys jumped to their feet. Coffee was forbidden at the Trading Post. Gramp said, "No coffee for growing boys." But here was Shemah offering them coffee and fried bread. They rushed to the kitchen. On the table was a basket of fried bread, small triangles of golden-brown, fat pincushions filled with air. Shemah poured coffee and refilled the basket when they had emptied it.

As they finished, Gramp came in. "Time to go," he told them. He did not notice the empty coffee cups, or perhaps he did notice them. Perhaps he too remembered that there was but a day left of this very special vacation.

They were going to a sing. Yellow-Shirt's-Son and Shemah went in the car with them. They never missed a sing—not if they could help it. Besides, this one was the Fire Dance. This was a ceremony no Navajo ever missed.

Yellow-Shirt's-Son was in a talkative mood. In the back seat where he sat with Shemah he kept up a sing-song monologue. Today he wanted to talk. Also, it was his duty to talk. It was his duty to tell these boys many things that they should know before they went away. He did not want them to go. He wanted them to stay here on the Reservation. It was where they belonged. It was where they should stay. But life trails were peculiar. They twisted and turned. They went into the far distance. He had seen them. He had watched those who had taken them. There was no straightening of trails. There was only the guiding in a good, strong way. This he would do. He would talk to the boys. He would tell them things that they should know.

"This Mountain Chant," Yellow-Shirt's-Son said, "is given when the thunder sleeps, before the thunder wakens in the summer. Not at any other time. This you know." His voice went on and on and on. "For nine nights and days," he said, "sand paintings are made, using the holy sand, following the holy way that the gods have so directed."

Yellow-Shirt's-Son stopped talking. He looked at the black head and the red head sitting in front. He wondered if the boys were listening to him. He doubted that they were. Still, he felt, he must keep on talking.

He said, "On the ninth night, this night that we are approaching, the dance of fire takes place." His voice droned on. No one listened.

Shemah's eyes were closed. She was thinking, My one, the dark one, will be content. He knows that for everyone there are two trails—the one he follows and the one he dreams about. But the small red boy must learn this. He thinks there is only one way, his way. He thinks those who do not walk it must be taught to walk it. He does not know that everyone must walk his own trail alone and in his own way. His Old Ones who have gone before him have not left for him this wisdom. Shemah's eyes opened. She looked at the two boys sitting in front of her. She thought, But the Old Ones have left the red boy something. They have left him courage to learn new lessons. Even though he learns through pain, he will learn them. The Indian woman smiled. The Old Ones know best what to leave behind them, she thought. It was a comforting thought. She closed her eyes again, this time in peaceful sleeping.

Hasteen thought of the new school. He thought of it with pleasure. Red wondered about Costa Rica. Would it in any way be like this? Were there Indians there? Would they be like the ones he knew? Would the Spanish people of Costa Rica be like the ones he knew who lived in the towns on the edges of the Reservation? Now that his going was all right with Gramp, Red could think with pleasure of what lay before him.

Gramp kept his eyes steadily on the road before him and wished that time could hold still and never change. Yellow-Shirt's-Son kept on talking, his voice a rich monotone.

Before long they reached the settlement of Two Rocks. The red canyon walls in the background jutted out to form two towering rocks like a gateway into an unknown beyond. At the foot of the rocks was a cluster of hogans where Dark Cloud, her husband Tall Man, and their small children lived. Hidden safely behind the rocks was the hogan of Dark Cloud's mother. She lived alone. Tall Man must never seem to see her, the mother of Dark Cloud, his wife. This the Ancients had directed—this the Navajos obeyed. It also had been decided by old ways that the hogan and the things of the hogan and the sheep flock belonged to Dark Cloud and not to her husband. Tall Man was content that it should be this way. His horse and his saddle were his. His turquoise and his concho belt belonged to him.

On the flat sand waste, sheltered on one side by the towering red rocks and on the other by stunted piñons and twisted cedars, were camped a thousand visiting Navajos. This was more than the usual number of visitors at a Night Chant. Many had come because of Yellow-Shirt's fame as a powerful medicine man, and also because of Dark Cloud's wealth. The Navajos had come in from all parts of the Reservation. Any ceremony under Yellow-Shirt's direction would attract visitors. Dark Cloud was wealthy and Tall Man was generous. He would see that many sheep were roasted, that much coffee was boiled, and that bread was plentiful. Dark Cloud had many sisters who would come to prepare the feast. All visitors would partake of the holiness of the medicine man and the hospitality of the hosts.

The boys were out of the car almost before it stopped. They circled the campfires. They visited at every wagon, car, and truck encampment. They exchanged greetings and gossip. They ate mutton and bread and drank strong, bitter coffee, not liking its taste but liking the grown-up feeling of being coffee drinkers.

The sun went down behind the red rocks, softening their outline, deepening their color. Shadows lengthened in the piñons. Dusk crept in among the cedars.

Close by, a ceremonial hogan had been built. People were drifting in and out of its doorway. The two boys drifted in with the crowd. Gramp was inside talking with Tall Man. When Red entered the hogan his grandfather looked sharply at him. The boy had entered the hogan correctly. He greeted his elders in a manner proper to his relationship to them. He sat where he should sit in a ceremonial hogan. Gramp sighed in relief and pleasure. The boy knew how to act. He knew how to accept the ways and the pattern of different groups of people. He would get along wherever he went. Gramp felt relieved. He had worried. Could Red accept the life ways of Costa Rica? Could he adjust to an entirely new pattern? Could he fit in without too much difficulty? Gramp decided that he could. May not be easy at first, he thought; his place was made for him here by his father and me, but he will make it in the end. Gramp's face shone with pride and affection for the young redhead, his grandson.

Yellow-Shirt, the medicine man, also looked up as the two boys entered the hogan. But his expression did not change. His eyes remained unreadable. No one could tell what he thought or whether his mind was emptied of earthly thoughts and filled only with the breath and the holiness of the gods. He looked down at his medicine bundle on the floor beside him. Red knew what was in it—an eagle plume, some eagle down, leaves and stems of holy plants, buckskin bags of sacred sand, yellow corn pollen and blue cornmeal. Red knew what they were. Many times had he watched Yellow-Shirt collecting them. But he made no sign that he had seen them before. Neither Hasteen nor Red, even by the flicker of an eyelash, seemed to recognize the old medicine man or his tools of magic and power. No one noticing the boys would know that for more years than they could count the holy man before them had been their teacher and their friend. No one could guess that the Old One had taught them to track and to hunt and to ride the sand trails of the desert land. No one could guess that it was he who had taught them, around the campfires, the hogan fires, the hearth fire, stories of the moon and the stars and the birds in flight. If he had recognized these boys in any way, the great medicine man in the ceremonial hogan would have broken a tradition and a trust.

The boys looked around the hogan. Dark Cloud sat on the sacred sand-painting. She looked tired and ill. The Night Chant was being given for her because she was ill—to make her well again. The boys did not speak to Dark Cloud, although they had known her for many years. She was not now a person whom they knew. She was part of a holiness that was outside everyday affairs.

The medicine man chanted his ancient prayers, brushing Dark Cloud with the eagle plume, sprinkling her with corn pollen. Red knew that before the night was over Yellow-Shirt would have performed his magic. He would have found the foreign objects or the hidden evil spells that had brought illness to Dark Cloud. He would have found them. He would have exposed them. He would have expelled them. Red knew, too, that afterward Dark Cloud would become well again. The boy had seen it happen again and again. He had never stopped to wonder if he believed in this or if Hasteen believed it. The Navajos believed in Yellow-Shirt. They believed in his magic and his power. The boy accepted their belief as natural and right and as something that belonged to them.

After a time, the two boys drifted out of the ceremonial hogan as quietly as they had drifted in. No one noticed them. They were part of the milling crowd.

Night came to Two Rocks. The stars hung low, warming themselves at the campfires dotting the sand flat. Two Indian men appeared at the doorway of the ceremonial hogan. They were attendants to the medicine man. They brought out the sacred sand that had been used in the sand-painting. They scattered it to the north, the south, the east, the west, to the sky, to the earth—the six Navajo directions to bless the Navajo world.

Close by, in the huge enclosure made by cedar-branch walls, a fire was built. There was no more talking among the thousand onlooking Navajos. There was no more feasting.

There was no more drifting to and from the ceremonial hogan and the cook shade. The night air became clearer, sharper, colder, shot through and through by an electric tenseness.

The people moved toward the enclosure. They did not move as individuals. They did not move in small groups. They moved as a mass, directed by one desire, in one direction for one purpose.

Then, to chanting no louder than the branch-brushed whisper of the wind, no louder than the dry-leaf rattle of the gourds, twelve men came into the circle of branches. Their bodies were painted with clay, gray, ghost-color, gleaming in the lights and shadows of the red-tongued flames. They carried wands that were tipped with eagle down. They performed feats of magic. They made a feather dance, standing upright in a Navajo meal basket. They made a stalk of yucca bloom, bursting forth in loveliness before the eyes of the onlookers. They made a cornstalk grow from a mound of sand. They left the circle in a mist of magic.

Only flames of the circle fire and the eyes of the watchers moved. The stars stood still. The tree stood still. The wind held its breath, and a thousand people waited.

Then into the circle of branches came twelve new clay-colored dancers. They came running. They came leaping, light-footed, light-bodied. They came swinging, swaying, scarcely touching the ground beneath their clay-painted feet. They sang the Fire Song. Like frenzied demons they sang the Fire Song. As they sang, they lighted shredded cedar bark from the flaming circle fire. They beat each other with the lighted torches. They tossed the flaming torches into the air and caught them as skillfully as one would catch a ball.

Men brought new wood for the fire. Its heat drove the onlookers back against the cedar-branch walls of the circle.

The dancers ran into the fire. They jumped through the circling flames and upon the glowing embers. The fire climbed upward in one last agony of flame.

Then suddenly the flames died to gray smoke, gray ashes. The dancers stopped. They moved away—gray figures moving lightly into a cold, gray dawn.

The sky became filled with sunrise colors. The thousand Navajos began to sing. They sang to greet the rising sun. They sang the Bluebird Song. Red loved the song. He knew it in Navajo. He knew its English meaning. He sang with the people:

> "Ah, ho, ho, ho, ho,
> Ee, hee, hee, hee yah, hee yah,
> Nah wee-nih, ha lith-nih,
> Nah wee, zahn, nih
> Nah, hah, yah
> Nah, hah, yah
> Nah, nah, yah."

The song was finished.

Although a thousand people sang it, their voices had blended with such sweetness, such beauty, that it became one sound, a living thing of sound.

The sky flamed in a moving mass of clouds as red as once the circle fire had been. The sun came forth, looking down on gray ashes, powdery, harmless, unreal.

As quickly as the fire had died, as quickly as the dancers had departed, as quickly as the sun had brought the day, the Navajos went their different ways. For a moment the men on horseback were black against the morning sky. Then they faded into the cool, blue distance. The wagons lumbered creakingly into the sand tracks and then vanished into a space of seemingly trackless sand. The cars and trucks left only a smell of smoke exhaust to tell that they had gone.

"From nowhere to nowhere," Gramp said, thinking of the thousand Navajos who had vanished into the morning. He covered the sleepy boys with blankets as they curled up in the back seat beside a sleeping Shemah.

"From here to the back of beyond," he said, starting the car toward the Trading Post and home.

Chapter Four

Red inched his head forward to see better. Cautiously, making no sound, he moved his cramped body. He was wedged in tightly between the vigas of the portal at the back of the Trading Post. Near him, stretching to the portal roof, was a magnificent lilac bush. It had been growing there for many years. Grandmother had planted it when first she came to the Trading Post thirty years ago. She had sheltered it from sand and wind. She had watered it during drought seasons when every drop of water had been precious. She had watched over it through the years with tender care. When

Grandmother died, Shemah had taken over. Her care was fierce and protective. Nothing must harm the lilac bush. Gramp called it the pride of the Trading Post and boasted that to his knowledge it was the only one on the Reservation.

Red was looking into its dark-green foliage with particular attention. This was not the first time the boy had spent peering into the lilac leaves. For the last two weeks he had spent many hours of every day wedged uncomfortably between the vigas, looking at a spot where a thick branch forked out from the main stem of the sturdy plant.

The lounging Navajos around the Trading Post had begun to tease him about the hours he spent under the portal roof. Gray Eyes asked him if he thought he was a bird, and Dawn Singer said, "No, the boy wants to be a viga on the portal roof." Only Yellow-Shirt understood his vigil. Yellow-Shirt told him not to listen to them, but to wait.

The day after Hasteen's departure for the Albuquerque school had been a long, long day. Red missed his friend more than he had thought possible. Always before it had been Red who had gone away and Hasteen who had stayed behind. Although Red had missed his friend each year when he returned to Middlebury, he now realized that it was easier to go than to stay. Going was filled with new things. Staying was an empty waiting.

At last the long day ended and the boy was glad when finally bedtime came and sleep filled the empty spot of Hasteen's going.

At dawn the next morning he was wakened by Yellow-Shirt. This was a surprise in itself. Yellow-Shirt never came into the house except at mealtime and to doze afterward before the hearth fire. Red could not believe it when he opened his eyes to see Yellow-Shirt bending over him. Yellow-

Shirt, who could speak English, but seldom did and never at length, motioned for the boy to follow him. It was cold and still outside with the coldness and the stillness of dawn. Yellow-Shirt squatted on the floor of the portal by the lilac bush and nodded for Red to sit beside him.

The old medicine man retreated into the folds of his blanket and sat motionless, waiting. Red tried to imitate the Old One and sit without movement, but he was cold, his teeth chattered, and he fidgeted. The old man seemed to have forgotten that the boy sat beside him. He neither spoke nor looked at him. He merely sat waiting. It must be five o'clock or even four o'clock, the middle of the night, Red thought crossly. He thought of the warm bed he had left.

Then he heard it, sweet and bright—the light, clear notes of the warbler's song. "Summer yellow bird, hear it? See it soon." Yellow-Shirt spoke softly so as not to mar the beauty of the song. Red remembered that was the Navajo name for the warbler. Anxiously he looked about him into the gray shadows of the morning. "Singing post," Yellow-Shirt said, pointing with his lips. Red looked. There on the post of Shemah's clothesline sat the golden bird, singing his heart out in his courtship song.

In the days that followed Red forgot everything, forgot missing Hasteen, forgot the coming great adventure of going to Costa Rica, in his excitement of watching the yellow warbler. The warblers had always been his favorite of all the birds he knew. They were so neat and small and graceful. They flew so high and sang so sweetly. But never before had he had the opportunity of seeing one so early in the season or at such close range. "I know him so intimately," he told Yellow-Shirt.

The old man answered, "He not afraid of you. He mean

something to you, maybe." The Old One nodded his wise, old head. "Could be," he said. "Who knows what birds know?"

As the days passed, Red had watched the warbler in his courtship with his lady bird. The bird sang and sang and sang from his perch on his singing post. Even the wash that Shemah hung on the clothesline near him did not daunt his singing. By the very sweetness of his song he tempted and coaxed and persuaded the bird of his choice to come nearer. He drove all rival birds away from his territory. The lilac bush was his, and he offered it to the rather drab little lady warbler for her nesting place. She flitted closer. She looked at the bush. She inspected it thoroughly. She liked what she saw and decided to stay.

Red was amused. "I think she likes the lilac bush better than she likes Mr. Warbler," he told Yellow-Shirt. The old medicine man was not amused. He was serious. "Yes," he said. "She does. It is their way—to choose their mate by the home he offers." It was a long speech for Yellow-Shirt—too long. He went away somewhere. Red watched the birds.

It was then that he found his hiding place between the vigas. There he could lie by the hour and watch the warblers make their nest. It took them four days, from dawn to dark, to make it. Mrs. Warbler did most of the work, but Mr. Warbler did what he could to help her. He flew by her side on all the trips she made, gathering bits of wool, thread, down, and leaves. He fed her as she worked and always, always, he sang to her. The bird made her nest cup-shaped. Settling her small, feathered body into it she smoothed and shaped it by turning around and around. The rim of the nest was made just so and to her liking. She smoothed it with a sideways motion of her wing tips and rounded it with her

neck, tucking twigs into it neatly with her bill. Now and
then the male bird sat in the nest. Red did not know if this
was to help smooth it or if Mr. Warbler's job was that of an
inspector. After four days the nest was completed to the
satisfaction of the two summer yellow birds.

Mr. Warbler went back to his singing post. His song was
softer, now that the frenzy of courting and nest-building was
over. He sang softly, sweetly to his mate to help her lay her
eggs. Monday, Tuesday, Wednesday, Thursday, Red counted
them. One egg each day the little lady bird laid in the felted
down of her tiny nest. The eggs were soft bluish white, with
a wreath of lavender and brownish markings around the
larger end. They were perfect and beautiful. Red said to
Yellow-Shirt, who had returned from some secret journey,
"I don't know which one of us is proudest of her eggs."

Yellow-Shirt smiled. He nodded with approval at the
eager boy. "All life is miracle," he told him. "Never forget.
Never forget importance of even small things coming to life."

Gramp grinned at his redheaded grandson. "Before long
you'll have the Old One talking as much as his son."

Red laughed. He remembered the night of the sing, and
how he and Hasteen had to close their ears against the talking of Yellow-Shirt's-Son.

Morning did not come soon enough. Night came too soon
for Red and his hourly watching of the summer yellow birds.
"I did not know that birds could be like this," he told his
grandfather. "Why, Gramp, they are like people."

Gramp nodded, chuckling as was his way. "And people
are like people. Redhead, you'll find that out wherever you
go."

After the eggs had been laid, there was a quiet time of
brooding. The mother bird was so careful and so patient.

The father bird was so anxious and so worried. Red thought it would never end. Eleven days he counted, watching, watching, watching the leafy heart of the lilac bush. For as long as he could watch through the long, long days, the mother bird sat in the nest and the father bird guarded her. He brought her tempting morsels of food and occasionally, but only occasionally, ate some of it himself.

At last the day came—the day of hatching. The boy lay between the vigas, looking down into the nest. He thought he could not bear the bursting wonder in his heart.

Then Gramp called to him. "Letters for you, Redhead. Look important to me." Red gave a slight wiggle, but he could not tear himself away. He dared not leave or call out that he was coming in a little while. This was the day, the moment, for which he had been waiting so long, so patiently. He must stay near the nest.

He looked. He watched. He saw an egg move ever so slightly. It bulged near the smaller end. Red saw it bulge. He held his breath. He dare not stir. Yellow-Shirt's-Son's voice rose high in the portal. "Come. Here are letters. Letters are to be read. How can letters to you be read if you do not read them?"

But now Red's excitement was so intense that he did not hear the high-pitched, calling voice. A half-minute passed. A minute passed. The egg moved again. It bulged again. It cracked. It broke. From the smallest end a tiny bird backed outward. It backed and pushed. The larger end of the egg cracked and broke. The bird's head was free. It was hatched. It was born. It wobbled on unsteady legs, scrawny, wet-looking, down-covered. Its eyes were closed, but even at this first moment of coming its wide, enormous bill was open hungrily.

How long had it taken? Red was not sure—two minutes, three minutes. Suddenly his muscles ached. Shemah was calling him now. "Come," her soft voice urged. "Your ancient grandfather wants you." Yellow-Shirt joined the callers. His voice was reassuring. He told the boy crouching in the vigas, "Tomorrow comes another bird."

Red looked quickly into the nest again. The mother bird was clearing her nest of the broken eggshell. The father bird had gone, but as Red looked he returned with something in his bill. This he put into the mother bird's mouth, and she in turn popped it into the open bill of the new baby warbler.

Red slid stiffly down the portal post. His red hair stood straight up, as it always did when he was excited. His freckles seemed to be popping from his face, and his blue eyes were shining. But only Yellow-Shirt understood the miracle of what the boy had seen and how deeply moved he was.

Gramp had a handful of mail, but the letter on top was the important one. He held it out to Red. "It's come," he said slowly.

Red knew what his grandfather was trying to say. He took the letter. It was from Mom, as he knew it would be. Slowly he opened it and read it. It said what he knew it would say.

Gramp asked, "When are you leaving?"

"Well, Mom doesn't say exactly," the boy answered, handing the old man the letter to read.

Gramp's face lighted. "You don't have to go tomorrow. That's good."

"I couldn't go tomorrow even if I had to," Red answered. "Before I leave here I've simply got to see the birds hatched out and watch them learn to fly."

"Twelve days birds gone," Yellow-Shirt said sadly.

Red looked at his letter again. "Mom says that it will be a

month before we go, but I should come home as soon as I can. Twelve days is as soon as I can.

His grandfather nodded. "Couldn't possibly get your plane reservation before twelve days," he said. He felt heavy-hearted, knowing that the time of the boy's departure was so final and so soon. Wouldn't be at all surprised, he thought, if our trails crossed down there in Costa Rica. My old bones sort of ache. Need a touch of tropic sun to make them young again.

The others drifted away. Only the old man and the young boy were left on the sun-warmed portal. "Aren't you going to read your other letters?" Gramp asked, handing the boy a second letter.

Red looked at it. "I almost forgot about it," he said. "Oh, Gramp, its from Hasteen. It's the first one he's written me since he got to his new school. I bet he has lots of news."

Gramp sat on the blanket-covered bench by the kitchen door. Red stood in the bright sunshine, reading the closely-written, small, penciled handwriting in the letter. "He likes it in Albuquerque," he said. "I knew he would. He planned to like it."

There was silence on the porch. The old man looked out at the red rocks. The little Desbah walked across the sand, herding her flock to the water hole. Every morning she herded them to the water hole; every evening she herded them back to the night corral. She never hurried. She never loitered. "As steady as time," Gramp thought. "As unchanging as time." He sighed. Two years, he thought.

Red gave an exclamation of unbelief. "Listen to this, Gramp. Listen to what Hasteen says." The boy began reading the letter aloud. " 'I wonder when my grandfather,' " he read, " 'will make me leave school and go into training to be a medicine man?' What does he mean, Gramp? What does Hasteen mean?"

"He means what he says," his grandfather answered. "I've always known that the Old One wanted the boy to follow in his footsteps. That's the Indian way."

"But his Indian way is to be an artist. He said so," Red protested.

"That's his personal Indian way. But to become a medicine man, if the Old One chooses him, will be his tribal responsibility," his grandfather explained.

Red looked at his grandfather. "Seems to me," he said, "Indians have too many responsibilities. They have more than we have."

His grandfather shook his head. "No," he answered, "not more. A different pattern, but not more. All life is linked with a chain of responsibilities, the person, the family, the group, and even between groups. The most important link of all is understanding." Gramp looked at his grandson. He spoke sharply. "Do you hear me, Red? Do you understand what I'm trying to tell you?"

Red's thoughts had gone back to the warblers' nest. "Um," he mumbled. "Even birds have responsibilities."

Gramp was disgusted. "You only part heard me," he grumbled. "You only half listened." The old man went into the Trading Post. He had work to do.

The next ten days passed swiftly. All the eggs were hatched now. The nest was full of hungry little birds. They were noisy, too, constantly peeping plaintively for food, food, and more food. One day, just for fun, Red clocked their feeding time. From five in the morning until after eight in the evening the parent birds flew back and forth, back and forth, bringing bill-fulls of food to their hungry family. The father fed the birds himself, now that they were older. It was only at first that he gave it to the mother bird to give them. "Fifteen hours," Red counted. "It must be a great responsibility to feed a baby bird." Then he grinned. "Next time a teacher or somebody says she eats like a bird, I might tell her something she doesn't know."

The boy never tired of watching the mother bird brood her young. In the mornings and at night she would fluff her feathers and bring her wings down close to the nest to give her babies warm, safe shelter. At noontime she stood in the nest with outspread wings to give them shade from a too-hot midday sun.

After three days of watching, Red saw the bulging, bright eyes open. But the little birds would close them tightly when they saw him looking at them. When he said, "Peep, peep," they would *peep-peep* back at him. Sure enough, just as Yellow-Shirt had said, along in the second week the parent birds began to coax the young from the nest. They called. They chirped. They coaxed. They scolded. For an entire day one little bird tottered on the rim of the nest, intending to fly, wanting to fly, but not being able to push himself to do it.

Red missed, somehow, the actual moment of flight. All at once he saw them flying. They were feathered now—pale olive bodies with brown wings edged and lined with yellow. Round, fat little bird-balls, they balanced themselves with their tails and were uncertain and wobbly and forever hungry. On the last day Red watched them the parent birds were still bringing food and dropping it into open, expectant bills.

The morning came for Red to go. It was not a sad time, as he had feared it would be. It was a busy time. Red had so

much to do. He had so many things and places and people
to tell good-by. "Buzzes around just like a mosquito," Yellow-
Shirt's-Son grumbled.

Shemah spoke sharply, not at all in her usual, soft manner.
"He who gathers along the way," she said in Navajo, "comes
not to trail's end empty-handed."

"Nor with an empty heart," the old medicine man added.

"Nor mind, I hope," Gramp said in English, getting into
the car. Red was the last one in. Gramp looked sharply at
him and then quickly away. Were those tear stains among
the freckles, he wondered. He thought they were.

For a while they rode in silence. Even Yellow-Shirt's-Son
seemed not to want to talk this morning.

But after a while Red spoke. "People are sure different,
aren't they Gramp? The people in Middlebury and the
Navajos here—they're just as different as they can be."

For a few minutes his grandfather did not answer him.
Then the old man sighed. "Well, yes, people are different,"
he said thoughtfully, "but people are people, too. There are
kinds and kinds. They have different folkways as groups.
They have common bonds, too, binding them together as
people."

Red was doubtful. He was not certain that he knew what
a "common bond" was.

"Language is a common bond," Gramp explained. "Perhaps it is the greatest. Common interests can be another
bond."

"Like things you give people, maybe. They could be a
bond," Red offered.

Gramp was not so sure of this. "Maybe," he said slowly,
"if the things you give have the same value to the people who
receive them—a common value."

"Um," Red said. He did not understand, but he did not want to admit it. Besides, he was too comfortable to want to know, to want to understand. It was such a good feeling to be riding along with his grandfather beside him. The Navajos in the back seat were quiet. Perhaps they were sleeping.

"Nice to be just us going to Gallup," the boy said drowsily.

"Nice," Gramp answered. He blew his nose and wiped his eyes. "If you were going to be gone more than two years I think I might miss you," he said huskily, trying to make a joke.

"Um," Red said, putting his head against the old man's arm. He closed his eyes just for a second.

After many minutes and many miles he wakened. They were coming into Gallup. They were nearing the airport. "Must have slept," Red said sheepishly.

Gramp laughed. "Here we are," he said. "Twelve noon, right on the dot. Time for a big lunch before the plane gets in."

At the airport counter a lump in the boy's throat kept him from swallowing the good food set before him. Panic filled him. "I don't want to go. I want to stay here. I don't want to leave you, Gramp," he said wildly.

"Nothing doing," his grandfather told him. "You're going on that new trail we've been talking about. Then you can tell me all about it soon as we see each other again. Wish I had your chance. I'd go so fast you couldn't see me." Gramp's voice sounded hearty and hale, but Red noticed that he had sugared his coffee a second time.

Yellow-Shirt and Shemah came looking for them. It was almost time to go. They spoke of little things to fill the hole that yawned before them.

Yellow-Shirt's-Son came in. He brought Red's suitcases and put them on the scales. Gramp had Red's ticket checked and handed it to him. The baggage was checked and wheeled away. The plane came in. The last good-bys were said.

Red looked very small as he went through the gate and up the steps into the plane. He did not look back. He could not. He did not stop to wave. The plane took off.

His grandfather looked around. He saw the red rocks of Gallup, the piñon-freckled hills, the windswept sand. He saw the Indians standing beside him, quiet, inarticulate in their sadness at parting. Their faces were closed. Their thoughts were locked deep within their hearts. They did not speak. They had no words.

Grandfather thought of the Trading Post, of the sheep and sagebrush. He thought of the Fire Dance at Two Rocks.

Grandfather thought of Middlebury, of its trim houses and its fenced lawns, of its boys' clubs and its schools and its churches.

All this has been his background, Gramp thought. This must be his measuring stick for the new life he is to enter, for the new ways he must learn to understand and to accept.

The plane was now a tiny speck against the vastness of the morning sky.

Chapter Five

"San José, Costa Rica!" Red exclaimed, looking downward from the speeding plane. "Central America! I didn't know it would look like this!"

How different it was! How different everything has been this time from that first trip when he had flown to his grandfather's! Then, he remembered, he had looked down on towns and people, highways full of trucks and cars, farms and the yellow sand country. On this trip, at first, they had flown high above the clouds, and Red could see nothing but a blanket of gray beneath the plane. Now all he could see was green, light feathery green, somber green, blue green, yellow green. He had not known that a whole land could be wrapped and bundled and smothered in green. Even when he closed his eyes it seemed as if green-tipped fingers were pressing against his eyelids.

How different was this jungle green from the world of the Navajo—that empty, barren, windswept, beautiful country. How long ago it seemed that he had been there with Gramp. And yet it had not been a long time, not a whole month ago.

On the plane trip back to Middlebury the boy had done a lot of thinking. His place at the Trading Post would not change. It would be waiting for him when he returned. His room, his museum, even his old jacket hanging next to Gramp's would be there waiting for him. When Shemah had not let him pack his old jacket he had been displeased. But no amount of coaxing would change her mind. "No," she had said, "not to take it. It stays here hanging by the Old One's jacket." Red was glad now. It was a comfort to think of the jacket hanging on the wall waiting for him to wear it again.

When he reached home nothing seemed torn up or displaced or unsettled. Clothing had been packed, but the furniture was as it always had been. Mom was renting the house while they were gone. There was routine—not the routine that he had known when his father was home and there had been no thought of ever leaving—but nevertheless a routine, a solid pattern of breakfast, lunch, and dinner, day and night.

It had been a quiet time, but also a busy time. It had been fun, too, feeling important with his friends and at club meeting. He was the boy who was going to a foreign country. It sounded exciting. It was exciting.

There had been last-minute shopping to do. There were inoculation shots to get at the Public Health Office. His passport came. Mom had let him take it to club meeting to show the other boys.

Even the last good-bys had not been bad. Not this time. Not for Red. Mom had cried—Mom, who almost never cried. But Red's heart was singing. At last, at last he was beginning the Great Adventure. Gramp did not mind his going—not too much. Gramp had wanted him to go. The boys who came to wave him good-by were as excited as he was. They wished they were going, they told him over and over. "Gramp would like to go, too," Red told them. "I'll tell you all about everything when I get back."

On the plane, at first, Mom had been afraid of flying. She had not said so, but Red had known. He who now was used to planes knew how it could be on one's first flight.

But all that had been a day ago. Now they were over Costa Rica. They had been flying over it for a long time. The plane swung low over a misting volcano crater. "Look, Mom, look! It's a volcano. It's real. It's active," Red whispered hoarsely to his mother who sat beside him. Wait until he told the boys at home! Boy! Was he glad he had come!

Occasionally there was a break in the jungle green. A river flowed—a thin, black line in the green background. At one place there was a tiny settlement, although no roads led in or out.

Gradually jagged mountains thrust upward through the verdant jungle. A wide valley opened out below. Cupped within, in fields of flowers, lay San José—a beautiful, gardened city, as unreal to the boy looking down upon it as a city in a fairyland.

Never again would any city seem to the boy to be as

beautiful and colorful as San José on that day of his arrival. The plane swung low over the flowered city and the green-covered hills creeping gently to its edges.

Never again was Red able to sort out what happened first or second or last. He remembered going through customs. Customs worried him. The men in customs examined his passport carefully. What if it had been made out incorrectly? The customs men went through his baggage carefully. Why were they looking so carefully? he wondered. There was nothing for them to find, nothing in his suitcases but his neatly folded clothing.

His mother, standing in line in front of him, seemed to be someone unfamiliar and unknown. A man closed the suitcases and motioned for Red to lock them. Then he stamped them, pushed them along, and looked at the redheaded boy. He smiled at Red. He said, *"Bueno."* He said, *"Pase."* Red forgot the little Spanish he knew. He did not understand a word. He moved along in the line because his mother in front of him was moving.

Someone handed him a cup of coffee. "Welcome to the coffee country," a man said in perfect English. Red looked at him. He was not a North American. The man smiled at him. "I am a Latin. I am a Tico," he said.

"Thank you," Red answered, not knowing what a Latin or a Tico was. He sipped the coffee. Suddenly he felt grown-up and not worried or afraid.

Then he saw his father, hurrying through the crowd to welcome them. How tall his father was, how broad-shouldered and big among the shorter, slighter men about him. Red greeted him. "You look so good and so American."

His father shook his head. "Not American. We are all Americans. Say North American, if that is what you mean."

The boy corrected himself immediately. He did not like to make mistakes.

Dad smiled at his son. "I've missed you very much. I need you with me." Red smiled with pleasure.

Soon they were in a taxi, rushing toward the city. It looked more like a fairyland than ever. Flowers of every kind, every size and color, crowded the wayside. Palm trees and bananas and pineapples grew in rows beside the road. Shining green coffee groves crowded close to the houses. The houses, too, were flower-colored, pink and yellow and violet and blue. They had arches and towers and balconies like little castles. In the openings of their high-walled enclosures were grilled windows and high, wide gates of wrought iron that looked like lace.

Finally the wide highway narrowed into city streets. Huge churches were almost on every block. In between were small shops with most of their wares spread out on the sidewalk before the iron-barred doors.

Everything was bright with color and gay with movement and noise. Buses were crowded with passengers. Taxis slithered around corners, their horns honking, their brakes screeching. Vendors swarmed the streets pushing vegetable-filled wagons or fruit-laden carts. The egg vendor, the bread man, the flower peddler, the ice man went along the streets singsonging their wares and how fresh and good they were. A man had a mule with huge milk cans tied to its fat sides. He and his mule went from door to door ladling out milk into pans, pitchers, and cups brought out to them. A man with a torch sat on the sidewalk, mending pans. A little servant stood by him, anxiously watching to see if he was doing it correctly.

Red tried to look in all directions at once. He tried to see everything. The taxi whizzed by great, patient oxen hauling heavy, creaking carts along the cobblestone streets. The wooden carts were beautiful. Their two sides and high, wooden wheels were painted in designs of many colors. Each cart owner had his own design. No one copied his neighbor. The huge, wooden wheels swayed and creaked.

"Need grease," Red told his father.

"No, they are supposed to creak. The Ticos call them singing carts. Each Tico knows the song of his own cart wheels."

"What is a Tico?" Red asked.

"It is the people's nickname for themselves," his father answered.

The taxi turned into one of the market streets. From wall to wall the street was thronged, crowded, packed with people and their wares. Red caught glimpses of tortoise-shell ornaments inlaid with mother-of-pearl; of alligator hides made into belts, boxes, bags, and shoes; of handspun rope and woven fiber hammocks; of articles of wood and leather, silver and clay, straw hats and baskets. He hung out of the car window as the driver slowly threaded his way through the crowded, narrow street.

At last they reached their destination. Red was amazed that his father had chosen this hotel. He was even more amazed when his father told him that it was the best one in San José. This was not like any hotel that the boy had ever seen in the states. Through the wrought-iron gates of the high wall around it the building looked old and faded. It was trimmed with all kinds of carved and scalloped woodwork. It had balconies and towers and flower boxes everywhere. It was old-fashioned and elegant, imposing and faded.

Young boys crowded around the car, asking, shouting,

pleading to be allowed to take the suitcases and bags into the building, but young men hurried out of the hotel, shooing and pushing the boys away. They loaded the baggage on their shoulders. Bellboys, Red thought. They were dressed in white, white shirts, white trousers, immaculate. Red took a second look. "Look! They're barefoot. Look, Dad, look! They're barefoot."

"Do you notice people's dress at home?" his mother asked quietly.

"Do you remark on the Indians' clothing?" his father said, his voice disapproving.

"I'm sorry. I didn't think. But they're so different." Suddenly the boy remembered his grandfather saying, "People are people." "I'm sorry," he said again.

The inside of the hotel seemed as un-hotel-like as the outside. There were no elevators. They walked up the broad, curving, thickly-carpeted stairs to their rooms. Red leaned over the marble banister to look down at the lobby. The high walls were lined with mirrors in ornamental gold-leaf frames. The high, narrow windows were covered with red velvet hangings reaching to the floor. From the high, vaulted ceilings lamps hung, dangling hundreds of rainbow-colored glass pendants. "Chandeliers," Mom called them. She kept murmuring, "How colonial! How elegant! How European!"

The large bedrooms were separated by a long room. Mom called it a drawing room. It looked like the lobby below, only smaller. Red went into the room Mom said was to be his. In one corner was a sort of fenced-up bathroom. Red was about to remark about it when he looked up at the ceiling. It was painted baby blue with rosy clouds and fat gold angels. The boy looked at his bed. The same gold angels were carved at its head and foot. He laughed out loud, thinking of Gramp and Hasteen and the bed rolls they used for camping trips. Mom and Dad came into the room. Mom's eyes were shining. Her cheeks were pink. "Isn't it lovely? Isn't it quaint?" she said. Dad winked at Red. Red grinned. Dad was the same. Costa Rica had not changed him.

"Hurry with your bath, son, and then we'll walk around the plaza," Mom said, unpacking a suitcase.

Dad went into the bathroom. Pointing to the faucets he said, "C is for *caliente*—hot; F is for *frío*—cold. Not like at home where C is for cold and H is for hot." He laughed. "Doesn't matter too much. There is never hot water anyway."

Red tried the C faucet, not believing that C was for hot. There was no water at all, either hot or cold. He tried the F faucet. Cold water gushed out. His bath felt fine.

They walked around the plaza. A band was playing in the bandstand. People sat or strolled about. Children played. Red was uneasy. "It's six o'clock," he said. "It must be six o'clock. We should eat. Dinner will be over."

His father laughed at him. "Dinner is at nine down here."

"Nine? That's my bedtime at home." He remembered the Navajo, where one ate when food was ready and slept when there was nothing else to do.

After their walk, they went into the hotel dining room. There was the same air of old-world elegance here as in the lobby and the rooms upstairs. At each place at the table there was a stack of plates. Red pushed his aside, all but one. He wished they would serve him quickly. He was afraid he was starving to death. The waiter put the plates back in a neat stack. Red was annoyed. His father shook his head, meaning, Red knew, "Let the waiter serve you in his way."

Finally food was brought in, served in courses. As each

plate at the top of the stack was emptied, it was whisked away. Each new course was served on the remaining top plate. There were soup, fish, fowl, beef, heart of palm, pineapple, and coffee. Red grinned, thinking of Shemah and the Reservation. "Hasteen would like it here," he said to his parents. He ate everything that was served him. "Wish there was another pile of plates," he told the waiter in English. The waiter answered in Spanish, and neither one was sure what the other had said.

Back in the rooms upstairs, servants flitted silently. They lighted the chandeliers and the tall, thin candles in the gold-leaf holders. They brought in tiny cups of much-sweetened coffee. Flower-scented air came in the open balcony windows. Church bells chimed, and the band still played in the bandstand in the plaza.

Red sat on the floor with his head against his mother's knee, listening to his father. Dad had found a house for them to live in near the cacao *finca* plantation, where he was working. It was called Hacienda Santa Maria and was the largest and the best house in that part of the country. The owner and his family were living in France. The hacienda was completely furnished. They would have the owner's servants and the owner's horses. Mom asked in alarm, "How many servants?" Red asked in pleased expectation, "How many horses?" Dad answered both questions vaguely. "It takes a lot of servants, down here, you know, and everybody rides horseback to places where they need to go."

Red was interested in the hacienda. He knew about the old southwestern haciendas. There was an old one at San Rafael, and he had gone there once with Gramp. It looked a lot like the Trading Post. It was adobe, long and low, with thick, whitewashed walls and viga ceilings. Red wondered if the people at Hacienda Santa Maria would be like the family at San Rafael. His thoughts wandered. He thought about Middlebury and the boys at school and about the college where his father taught. He thought of Gramp and Hasteen and the lonely, beautiful Reservation. They are so different, he thought. Then he remembered his grandfather saying, "People are people." He felt comforted again.

His father was saying, "We leave in the morning. The only way to get there is by train."

His mother said, "Way past your bedtime, Red."

The boy felt at peace and very sleepy.

Chapter Six

Red was wakened by a little maidservant pushing a table just big enough for one beside his bed. The servant, chatting happily in Spanish, brought a large, silver pitcher of heated milk, a small, silver pitcher of cold coffee essence, and the largest, deepest silver sugar bowl the boy had ever seen. She made coffee—a small cup half filled with sugar, some hot milk, and a few drops of the black, thick, syrupy essence. She brought warm orange juice, a dish of jam, and a basket full of hard-crusted rolls of many shapes. This was breakfast. Red ate it, wishing for the oatmeal, sausage, and hot-cakes he had for breakfast in Middlebury.

After breakfast there was great hurry and flurry and hustle and scurry in getting Mom and Dad and Red and the luggage downstairs and into a taxi. The taxi speeded and swayed down the early-morning streets to the railroad station.

Yesterday the marketplace had been crowded, but it was nothing compared with the number of people at the railroad station. When the taxi stopped people swarmed upon it— beggars, vendors, shoeshine boys, porters. Dad chose several porters to carry the baggage. Then, following them, he pushed a way through the crowd for Mom and Red to get to the train. Their car was first-class, so it was not crowded, but dozens and dozens of people climbed into the second-class cars. Mom was breathless, and even Dad was panting.

"Our tickets, our tickets! You forgot to get our tickets," Red shouted above the noise of the crowd.

His father shouted back to him, "Don't need tickets. The Costa Rican government has given us passes on their National Railroad."

"Why?" Red shouted. "I didn't know they even knew you."

Their car was quiet now, since most of the people had boarded the other cars. Dad said in his usual tone, but with a twinkle in his eye, "They know me. I'm helping to solve some of the cacao problems."

Red was surprised to think that the Costa Rican government knew that his father was here!

The train left at the scheduled time. "Right on the dot," Dad said. "The buses leave when they are full, early or late, but the trains leave on time."

The train gained speed at once. It swayed and bumped and rattled and tooted. Mom sat with her eyes closed, but Red and his father talked with each other above the din.

"Men from the States laid out this line. Young fellow by the name of Keith, Minor Keith," Dad said. "There were a hundred laborers' lives lost for every mile of track that was laid."

Red could believe this. The train hung by a track width to mountain edges and swung crazily over deep, dark chasms. It dashed high above turbulent dark-green rivers. It skirted waterfalls so closely that spray came through the open windows of the cars. It sped through high mountain valleys where velvet-soft, flower-studded grass spread park-like on every side.

After a while the train began its descent, turning, twisting, speeding down the mountainsides. At last it entered what Red thought was jungle. "Not jungle," Dad told him, "not yet. This is called bush country." But to Red it was jungle—deep, dark, shade-filled jungle where trees pressed closely, almost touching the little train as it shot by.

At noon they stopped in a clearing. There were a few houses here—built high on stilts, thatched with straw. At once the little settlement that had been sleeping while it waited for the train came awake. At once all the house doors were filled. Women and young girls glided down the ladder steps. They ran across the clearing. All of them ran with the same gliding movement. It made them seem like birds flocking to a water hole. Their skirts swished. Their bright blouses fluttered. Their small, bare feet touched lightly the moss-thick grass. The baskets on their heads tilted but did not tip or fall from where they perched on the shining, coiled, black braids.

The women and girls came to the open windows of the train, calling, talking, laughing, making a lot of noise. Red stretched out to look down into their baskets, which were filled with bananas, oranges, limes, and mangoes. There were other baskets full of little bundles wrapped in banana leaves. There were baskets of rice and roasted chicken and pork pieces and roasted yams. There were baskets of rolls like the ones Red had eaten for breakfast that morning. Right beneath him was a basket of hunks of yellow sponge cake. There were other baskets of eggs. Red held his breath as a little woman wearing a basket of eggs ran gaily by the car windows singsonging what she had to sell. Right behind her walked a basket-lady with a coffee pot, a pitcher of milk, and a stack of cups. All the women balanced their baskets on their heads without holding them or even touching them with their finger tips. They ran. They laughed. They bargained. They gestured with their hands and not a basket fell.

Mom and Dad had a long conversation about what to buy and what not to buy. Red was so hungry he would have liked everything in every basket. He looked out at the string of cars ahead. Dusty, hungry passengers were hanging out of the windows. They were gesturing, arguing, bargaining, and at last buying the foods the women offered them. There was much good-natured chattering, scolding, laughing, joking, as the women bargained and the passengers bought.

Red was dizzy from the sounds and smells and sights. He also was hungry. "Quit talking, Mom, and buy something. I'm starved."

Dad opened his mouth to correct his son's voice and language. Instead he surprised even himself by saying, "Me, too. I'm starved. I could eat anything."

Mom chose bananas, pineapples, oranges, and yams. She

said, "I'm buying the things we can peel. That's what the book says to do."

Red saw his father look at the chicken and rice and glance quickly away. He's as hungry as I am, Red thought, quietly buying two rolls and two wedges of cake from the basket nearest him, and he and his father ate them to the last good crumb.

Finally all the passengers in all the cars had bought all the things they wanted to buy. The brakeman waved to the engineer to start the train. With a lurch it whistled and rattled into the green distance that closed in upon it on every side.

By midafternoon the train reached Puerto Limón, the end of the line, the end of the track. It had reached the sea. Puerto Limón, a busy seaport, was a tropical lowland city. The air smelled of flowers, of plant life, dense and thick, of rich, damp earth and of ocean spray. Puerto Limón was a city of flowers and tall, proud trees, ornate white buildings, and tall, black people.

Red stood with his mother and father on the station platform, their luggage piled high around them. Red was excited. "Are they Spanish?"

Mom was excited, too. "How far is it to the hacienda? I want to get there. I want to get settled."

Dad tried to answer both of them at the same time. "I had planned to have us stay here for the night. No, they are from Jamaica."

Mom repeated her question. "How far is it to the hacienda?"

Red said, "Do they speak English or Spanish?"

Dad was growing impatient. "They speak both, I imagine. English is their mother tongue. They are British subjects."

And to Mother he said, "We must go the rest of the way by jeep. We could not possibly get to the hacienda tonight."

"Where's the next town?" Mom asked.

Dad hesitated. "There is a way station about four hours away. We could stay there, I guess."

Mom sat down on the luggage. "Get the jeep, Patrick," she said. When Mom called Dad "Patrick" she meant what she said. Red would have liked to stay in Limón for the night. He had never seen a seaport town before, but he knew better than to coax when Mom was like this.

The boy saw a park not far away. "May I go walk in the park while you get the jeep?" he asked his father.

"Yes," his father said. His mother said, "No."

Red did not hear her. He ran across the busy street.

The park was cool and shadowy and very beautiful. Stately royal palm and tall cocoanut trees swayed their lofty heads in a breeze from the sea. Red knew what the trees were because he had seen pictures of them and had read about them. But the plants and vines and ferns and flowers growing along the paths were new to him.

Little black boys ran around, playing and shouting. It made Red feel gay and light-hearted just to look at them. He bought peanuts from a peanut vendor, paying for them shyly with Costa Rican money.

He reached the seawall. There was the sea!

Middle West and Southwest were what he had known. He never had seen the ocean so close before, although he had seen lakes. Lake Michigan was not far away from home in Middlebury. Red had not thought much about oceans until now. Now he had his first awakening to a knowledge of the force and the power and the grandeur of the sea.

He leaned against the seawall, looking at the waves breaking in relentless, hopeless fury against the unyielding wall. They never stopped. They never paused. Slap, slap, slap they went, accompanied by a sad and muted roar.

An old man came to stand beside him. "Caribbean," he said. His voice was low and musical and filled with pride and love and longing.

Red looked at him in surprise. "You love the sea as I love the desert," he said softly. The old man nodded. Red felt close and friendly to the stranger beside him. The old man and the young boy leaned against the seawall and were lost in thought and understanding.

Someone tapped Red's shoulder. Startled, he looked around. A tall man dressed in khaki stood beside him. "Your father has said for you to come. We are about to start on our journey to the hacienda," he said in English. Red looked where the man had pointed. There were two jeeps waiting. One was a jeep truck and in it was their luggage. The one they were to ride in was a "jeepster." Mom was sitting in the front seat. She looked frightened. She had never been in a jeep before. She knew she was not going to enjoy being in this one.

Red followed the tall man across the street. "This is Señor Ramón, Red," his father said, nodding toward the tall man. "He works with me in the cacao experiments. And this is Quaco," he said, pointing to a young Jamaican who would drive the truck.

Both men shook Red's hand with the same courtesy they would show if Red had been a man instead of a boy. Red liked them instantly. He would have liked to ride with Quaco and get acquainted, but suddenly he felt too shy to ask his father if he might do so.

Señor Ramón got into the driver's seat beside Mom. Red

climbed into the back with his father. They began the last lap of their journey to their new home.

Red grinned. "We sure skimmed through Limón."

His father laughed.

The road was narrow and moss-covered. The trees pressed closely together, making a roof of branches overhead. Except for the bouncing jeep, the whole world seemed to stand still beneath the heavy heat of the ending day. Jasmine hung their fragrant heads in wilted weariness. Orchids—lilac, purple, yellow, and cream-colored—closed their loveliness to the coming night. Red said he heard a dog bark somewhere.

Dad shook his head. "Not a dog, a howler monkey. You will see them at the finca."

Macaws—red, blue, yellow, black, and white—flew in lazy pairs, making spots of color in the leafy green.

A bush in front of them seemed covered with blossoms, but when the jeep came beside it the blossoms rose in midair, a cloud of butterflies. They were huge. Their tawny wings were edged in velvet black. "Monarchs," Dad explained. "They are the butterfly dandies. Can you see that black patch on their legs? It's a black satchel full of perfume to please the lady butterflies."

Red beamed at his father. "You know as many interesting things as Gramp does," he said approvingly.

His father looked pleased. He would have liked to be like Gramp in every way. Even as a boy he had longed to be like his sparkling, redheaded father. But he had not been. He had been dark and quiet and serious. Spurred on by the compliment his son had given him, he began talking about the butterflies they had seen. "The monarch is the only butterfly that can fly over the sea. That's why it can migrate. Those we saw today must be migrating."

Night monkeys moaned. Parakeets fretted. Birds began
to hum their evening prayers. Would they look like the birds
of home? Red wondered. He strained his eyes to catch sight
of some sleepy feathered fellow, but all he could see were
leaves of green hiding their secret world. He told his father
about the warblers he had watched at the Trading Post.
"They are my favorite birds," the boy confided. "Are there
warblers here?"

"I haven't seen any," his father answered. "But there are
other birds you might get to like as much as warblers."

The jeep shuddered to a stop. Nesting among the trees
was a bungalow built on stilts. There was a flower garden
in front with a picket fence around it and a swinging gate.
"Looks like a house in Middlebury except for the stilts,"
Red whispered to his father as he climbed from the jeep.

The house had steep steps leading up to its door. At the
top an old man and woman stood, calling down to welcome
them.

"English people," Dad said as he helped Mom up the steps.
"Martha and Gerald Smythe-Hayes, right out of an English
novel. They've been here for twenty years or more, keeping
the way station open for every stranger who passes by."

"Like Gramp at the Trading Post," Red said in a flash of
homesickness.

Inside the bungalow the rooms were bright with chintz
curtains and pillows and braided rag rugs. On one wall was
a gilt-framed picture of Queen Victoria. Mom began to cry.

Martha Smythe-Hayes comforted her. "There, there,
dearie, I know how it is. I know what you're going through.
You'll get to like it, once you know it. And anyway, you'll
always find a spot of England here to welcome you."

Red was tired and hungry. At the supper table the food

was strange, but it was good. He asked for second helpings.

Afterward he went to bed in a small screened-in room high above the flower garden and on a level with the whispering trees. His bed reminded him of the one at home—narrow, soft, and comfortable. He fingered the patchwork quilt. It was like the one he had, the one his grandmother had made for him.

Night came swiftly to the clearing in the brush. Tall cacao trees in the old groves swayed gently in the cooling breeze. In the new groves, the fast-growing palm oil and gum trees bent gently above the cacao seedlings to shelter them from the winds of night.

The clearing where the Smythe-Hayeses lived was quiet. Perhaps it dreamed of ages past, before men came, when it was wild. Then the trees had grown thickly, much more thickly. Bushes and thickets walled the tree growths. Vine branches met and tangled overhead, and the sun never shone on the damp, dark earth. Only the raindrops and the whispers of wind could seep through the dense walls of growing green.

That was before men had come to the brush country. It had changed with their coming—a little. A road had been built. A settlement had been cleared. Men came and stayed and waged eternal war against the growth that crept day and night across his roads and through his clearings. Man cut and burned incessantly, and the plant life of the dark brush country seeded itself and grew across the wounds that civilization had made upon the land.

But Red did not know this. He did not know of the eternal warfare between man and nature. As he lay in his narrow bed it seemed as if this were a world without people. It was a world in its beginning. Men had not been here.

They had not tamed this land. The trees had no names. The rivers had no names. There were no towns. Middlebury had never been, and the Navajo Reservation was in another world.

It had been a long and unbelievable day.

Chapter Seven

Mom was happy this morning. In a few hours she would reach her new home. She was anxious to get there, to see what it was like, to start making it into what she wanted it to be. Mom had never admitted it, but two years seemed a long time to her, too. She knew that it could be just a break in the pattern of their lives or an experience that would enrich them forever. She was determined to make the time a serene and rewarding one for her husband and her son. First, last, and always Mom was a homemaker. She loved her home. She loved making it attractive and inviting, a restful and a happy place. She loved entertaining. There were always guests; for an hour, for overnight, for a week, whenever they came she made them welcome.

As a faculty wife she was loved for her hospitality to both old and young. College students made her house their second home. Members of the college faculty ran in and out with neighborly freedom. She was known for the casual, comfortable, informal living that was part of her homemaking.

None of their friends had servants. Wives in Middlebury prided themselves on doing what needed to be done without hired help. They prided themselves in being able to cope with all the emergencies of daily life. Mom could cook and sew, clean house, and tend her garden. She was the family banker, the family handy man, the family chauffeur and, when need be, the family nurse.

Mom was happy and gay and pretty. She was firm, which was all right. She was very dear to her husband and her son.

They were happy this morning, because she was happy. Dad was relieved that she had come. He needed her. Red was just happy because Mom was happy. He knew without thinking about it that everything would be all right because she was here.

They reached the hacienda in midafternoon. They had eaten no lunch. There had been no place to eat. Red wondered if there would be a snack of any kind in the refrigerator. Mom wondered if there would be a refrigerator.

They arrived at enormous wrought-iron gates. Above them was a painted sign: HACIENDA SANTA MARIA. Quaco got out to open the gates, and Red hung out of the jeep for the first glimpse of his new home. There was a wide, curving driveway shaded by massive ancient trees. Red saw in the distance a white dovecote and a fountain and a pool. The place was a riot of blossoms. Mom cried out in pleasure. She was as eager as the boy in the back seat to see what the next curve would bring.

But when they saw it, it did not look as Red had thought it would. It was not low, or long, or built of sun-dried bricks. It was an almost square, high, two-story frame house surrounded by two-story porches and almost smothered in flowering vines.

On the front steps, to welcome them, stood a small crowd of people. Red thought they were neighbors until he heard his father say, "These are your servants, Mollie."

The inside of the house looked strange and formal to the boy who had pictured a long, low, thick-walled room bright with Indian blankets and a blazing open fire. There was no fire or fireplace, nor any kind of heating stove. Everything smelled of dampness. The rooms were high-ceilinged and paneled in mahogany, a luxury few houses in the States could afford. But they were dark. The carved furniture was massive, and richly upholstered in crimson velvet. But it was stiff-looking, uninviting.

The house was not as Mom had pictured it, but she was not discouraged. With her quick, practical mind she planned the changes she would make. This she decided was something she could do—bring a bit of Middlebury into a strange and foreign land. The number of servants, however, frightened her. She kept saying, "But what will I do with so many of you?"

There were many, at least many for a woman who had never had a servant. Red tried to get them straightened out. The old, fat one was Lin, a Chinese, the cook for the hacienda. Red grinned at him, liking him immediately. He looked like a roly-poly Hopi Indian. There were Carmencita, the housekeeper, and her daughter Marita, the housemaid. There were Tio, the gardener, and José, who helped him. Juan, an older man, was with the others. Red did not know what he was supposed to do. Juan had a son, Juanito, a boy Red thought about his own age. Juanito stayed in the background, not unfriendly, but not friendly either. Red tried to get acquainted, but the boy did not understand English or, apparently, Red's halting Spanish.

Red said, "Let's eat. Let's ask Juanito to eat with us." This reminded Mom that her duties as lady of the house had begun. When she went into the kitchen she was surprised to find a hearty meal being kept warm for their coming. Mom was delighted. She was delighted with the quick, smiling graciousness of these people who wanted to serve her. She said softly, "*Gracias.*" This was her first Spanish speech in her new home.

Red was disappointed, when food was ready, to learn that Juanito was nowhere to be found. "He's shy," his father told him. "Give him time to get to know you."

Tomorrow, Red promised himself. Tomorrow I'll make friends with Juanito.

He did not know how many tomorrows and tomorrows would pass before the shy Costa Rican boy would accept him as a friend.

The next few days passed quickly. Red was interested in everything. He quickly found that Lin, the Chinese cook, was a fund of information. "Where are the Indians?" Red asked. "I thought there would be many Indians, and I haven't seen a one."

Lin laughed. Red soon learned that laughter was part of Lin's conversation. He began and ended every conversation with laughter. "No Indians." He laughed now. "No Indians in bush country. Some in the jungle. You be good boy someday maybe I take you."

Red was not satisfied. "But why aren't they around here? Why are they in the jungle?"

"No like." Lin chuckled. "Few left. Someday maybe I take you."

Red asked another question. "Where are the cowboys? Costa Rica raises cattle. I read about it."

"No cowboys in bush country. Some in Guanacaste. You be good boy, someday maybe I take you."

Red missed having other boys around. Secretly he was very disappointed that there was to be no school for him. At first his father had planned that he would go to school at San Ysido, the nearest settlement. There were a few children, a small schoolhouse, and a teacher there. "He will make friends in no time at all," Dad promised Mom when they were talking about it. But when father had planned, he had not known that marsh lands, an unbridged river, and bush-country growth lay between the hacienda and the settlement. The settlement was on the railroad, but train schedules were uncertain and not every day. There was no road. There was not even a foot trail. San Ysido was a nearby dot on the map, but it was impossible to get there.

Although Red could not go to school, he would not miss lessons. Mom said she would begin teaching him on the first of September. Red knew that he would keep up, after a fashion, with the boys at home. These two years would not be lost years. There would be many things he would learn besides chapters and lessons in textbooks. Red understood this. But school meant so much more than textbooks. School meant companionship. It meant planning things and doing things with other boys. It meant sharing experiences and opinions. It meant living in a boy's world.

He needed a friend. He needed Juanito. Red always had made friends quickly and easily. In Middlebury it had been the same school, the same club, the same neighborhood, children of his parents' friends. On the Navajo Reservation it had been Gramp and Hasteen, the old medicine man and his son and Shemah. But here it was different. Juanito and Red had neither background nor customs nor friends in common. They spoke different languages. If Juanito spoke English as Hasteen did, Red thought, then my poor Spanish would not matter. But Juanito spoke no English.

At night Red memorized sentences to say in Spanish when he met Juanito in the morning. Juanito was courteous. He tried to understand Red's Spanish. He tried to make his Spanish answers slow enough for Red to understand them.

"You need to learn Spanish quickly, Red. You need to think in Spanish," his father told him.

"I know," Red said sadly, "but even if I could speak it I can't think of anything to talk about in Spanish."

His father was sympathetic but not helpful. "It is something you will have to work out for yourself."

Red knew this. One way to work it out was to make friends with Juanito. He was determined to do so.

One day he gave the Costa Rican boy a marble. It was his prettiest one, and he hated to part with it. Juanito was pleased. He kept saying in Spanish, "Very pretty, very pretty, thank you." Red did not know that the Coast Rican boy had never played marbles, that he did not know what marbles were for.

That afternoon Juanito gave Red an empty bottle. Red took it, turning it over and over. He said politely, "This is a

good, strong bottle. Thank you. Thank you very much."
But he did not know exactly what to do with it. He did
not know that at Hacienda Santa Maria an empty bottle was
a treasure, difficult to come by.

Mom fitted into her new home quickly. It had not taken
her long to get used to having servants. She exchanged
recipes with Lin, who did not mind having such a gracious,
pretty lady come into his kitchen. She and Carmencita spent
happy hours making over some of Mom's dresses to fit the
little maid, Marita. Juan was the handy man at the hacienda.
He was the man-of-all-work, finding things to keep himself
busy. He was now building a springhouse over a spring so
that Mom could have the refrigerator she seemed to want
so badly.

The flower garden was beautiful, and day by day it became
more beautiful. Mom spent hours with Tio, showing him
what to transplant and where to transplant it. Daily she
chose armfuls of flowers for Tio to cut and Carmencita to
take into the house to brighten its dark corners.

Mom was happy—or almost happy. She worried about
Red. Red was lonely—Red who had never lacked friends
and things to do with them.

Rain came daily. The boy spent hours sitting on the porch,
looking out at a world of glistening, rain-washed loneliness.
His mother tried to interest him in her garden. She was
especially proud of her orchids. She pointed them out to
her son. "See this one, Red, this purple one. It is the national
flower of Costa Rica." Red looked; dutifully he fingered the
delicate blossom. Mother pointed to another one. "And this
one, son. Look at its center. Isn't it the perfect image of a
dove? It's called the Holy Ghost. This one is called White
Nun."

Red was polite but indifferent. He would have traded all of them for Gramp's geraniums that grew in pots with their roots in the earth.

If he had work to do, Mom thought; chores like those he did at home . . . But there was no work for the son of the Hacienda master. There were servants who did the work. Carmencita cleaned Red's room. Marita tended his clothing. Juanito shined his shoes. The kitchen belonged to Lin, the garden to Tio. Juan was the chore man. There was nothing for Red to do.

There were saddle horses at the finca. Red loved to ride. His father said, "The horses need exercise. You and Juanito ride them. I will send Quaco with you."

Red was delighted. They would ride together. They would explore the countryside together. They would take bedrolls with them, a pack horse or two, and camp. He knew all about camping. He had learned to ride and to camp almost as soon as he had learned to walk.

At first this looked as if it might come true. The boys rode every morning and came back at noon drenched with the daily rains. They saw parrots and macaws, and once two white cockatoos flying together. Sometimes they caught a glimpse of monkeys and always they heard their noisy chatter. Often they saw alligators sunning themselves on the bank of the river. But they never saw enough.

Red wanted to see more. He wanted to get down from the safety of his saddle and hide in the fern bank and watch and wait for more. Quaco would not allow him to dismount. "Snakes," he said shortly. There were no side journeys off the mossy road, no matter how inviting a cleared way might look. Quaco would not allow it.

The morning ride was always the same way, down the

road to the clearing and back again. There was no exploring. Boys do not explore the bush country of tropical lands. There were no foot trails. Riding was limited to the road, and the road was a short one.

Each morning Quaco and Juanito led the horses up the hacienda driveway. They stopped by the fountain at the front veranda. Quaco held Red's horse for Red to mount it. When he was safe in the saddle, the other boys mounted their own horses. This embarrassed Red. He did not like to be waited on or waited for. He knew their doing so was custom, but even so it made him feel awkward and ill at ease.

Each noon, when they had finished riding, Quaco held Red's horse for him to dismount. Then he and Juanito led the horses away. Gramp always said, Red remembered, that a fellow who did not take care of his own horse should be made to walk. He had taught Red to water and feed his horse, to brush and curry it, to saddle it, and to bed it down. Red wanted to do these things as he had been taught to do them. He wanted to take care of his own horse. Quaco would not allow it. He seemed horrified that Red would want to do such work. He seemed ashamed that the boy knew how. Red's Spanish was not fluent enough for him to explain that a North American boy is taught such work, that he wants to do it. Besides he doubted that even fluency with words would make Quaco understand.

The rides became less frequent. At last they stopped altogether. Quaco went back to his regular job of driving the jeep for Dad and Señor Ramón. Juanito disappeared. Sometimes Red saw him working with his father or with Tio. There was always work that Juanito could do. He was the handy man's son.

Red sat on the veranda again, looking at the green-walled world.

Mom became desperate. "You have to do something," she told the boy's father. "It isn't like Red to sit around all day."

"I could take him with me to the groves," Dad said. "I'm busy, but he could amuse himself."

So it was decided that the boy would go with his father each day to the clearing and out from it to all the cacao groves.

Red was pleased. He was excited. It was something to do. He could explore the groves and get to know the workers. He could talk with them. He could ask them questions about cacao. They would understand his Spanish. He knew he could make them understand it. He could help them work. He could learn how to do what they did.

The evening before he was to go was long and dull, and even the night was wakeful, as he waited for morning to come—morning and something to do!

Chapter Eight

Red climbed into the back of the jeep. His father got in
front with Señor Ramón, who had come for them. Marita
came running from the house, bringing their noontime lunch
—three neat little bundles wrapped in plantain leaves. Mom

waved good-by from the doorway. Señor Ramón started the jeep.

It had rained almost all night. Early-morning mist swirled about them, hiding the house completely before they had reached the curve in the tree-shaded driveway.

Red was glad that Dad had said that he could go with him today. Dad had said that Red should know about his new home, and that he should go every day until he knew everything, or almost everything, there was to know. Red agreed with him. He was eager to learn.

Rain began again. It did not fall in drops as it did in Middlebury, or in an angry downpour like cloudbursts on the Navajo. It sifted gently down like a lace-fine spray. Red stuck his head out from the cover of the jeep to feel the rain upon his face and to sniff the perfumed world.

The jeep passed through a clump of bamboo that grew tree-tall, with jointed woody stems. Red's father called back to him, "Deer," pointing to a vague, shadowy something feeding among the bamboo shoots. Red looked in surprise. These deer were small, much smaller than those on the Reservation.

Before long they reached the clearing where the cacao workers lived. There were perhaps a dozen houses, all alike, all the same size. They had walls of bamboo and roofs of plantain leaves. They stood high off the ground on stilts made of stout poles. In the open enclosures beneath the houses pigs rooted and chickens drooped and thin dogs scratched their fleas. Under one house two fighting roosters jumped at each other, pecking viciously, spurring without mercy and flapping their wings. Fine dust rose in a cloud around them although the world outside glistened with silvery rain.

The clearing seemed deserted. "Where are the people?" Red asked, climbing out of the jeep almost as soon as it stopped. He stood beside Señor Ramón, seeing everything he could see in the misting lights.

"Working," Señor Ramón answered.

Dad turned away, saying, "I want to talk with Papacito." He went toward a huge aluminum warehouse at the edge of the clearing.

"Who is Papacito?" Red asked.

"He is the headman of the village," his father answered. "He was the first African to come to this locality. Where he came from exactly or why he came I do not know." Father walked along slowly, talking as he walked. Red tagged along beside him, fearful of losing a word. "He came here with his young sons," Dad continued. "They cleared the brush and felled the trees and cut and burned the underbrush. Then they planted seedling cacao."

Red's father stopped to catch his breath. Señor Ramón took up the explanation. Pointing to the trees growing beside the cacao plants, he said, "They planted these gum trees—madre-de-cacao, mother of the cacao they are called —to shade and protect the seedlings. They built their houses. These that you see here are ones very much like the first houses that were built here."

On the far side of the warehouse stood the store. "Like a trading post," Red said, pleased that here was something that was almost familiar. "Did Papacito build it?" Red asked.

Señor Ramón answered, "No, a banana company built the store and the warehouse. They buy the harvested cacao from the people who live here in the settlement."

"Papacito and his sons?" Red asked.

Señor Ramón nodded. "Papacito and his sons and their families," he said. "The Costa Rican government," he added, "and the banana company ask people like your father to come here to make a study of cacao and its future development."

"Wait here, Red," Dad said. "I will find Papacito, and we will come back for you."

Red looked around at the quiet, deserted clearing. Year after year men had fought insect enemies of the cacao they had planted. They had fought the thieving birds, the vandal monkeys, and the plant diseases. They had fought the jungle plants that incessantly crept closer, closer to take back the man-planted groves into the wilderness again.

Cacao planters were never finished. They could never look back at what had been accomplished. There was no time. Cacao planters must be forever fighting. Incessantly they must fight the creeping jungle.

Red did not think these thoughts in words. He felt them. He had a new awareness of what some men must do to give other men things that are taken for granted. Men had died here and other places like it so that boys like him could have cocoa for breakfast and chocolate cake for lunch.

Papacito came with Dad and Señor Ramón. They climbed into the jeep. Papacito sat in front this time and Dad in back with Red.

First they went to the seedling groves. They watched the men and boys at work planting the seedlings. Some of the boys looked no older than Red who watched them. They were not boys, he thought, not boys like the ones he knew and played with at home. These boys were men, doing men's work. They were dressed in white shin-length trousers, shirts with shirttails flapping as they bent to plant. Men and boys worked together in a rhythm of movement, taking five or six seeds from a pod and placing them in shallow holes five or six yards apart. The whole group worked without sound, without speech.

"Next year these seedling plants will be transplanted to a new clearing," Dad explained. His voice seemed unusually loud in the silence around them. Red did not answer. He kept his look fixed on the boys working so intently. When they had finished here they would go to the old groves to weed, to cultivate, to spray.

Señor Ramón parked the jeep. They would walk the rest of the way, the rest of the day. They went first to last month's seedling beds, where new plants were growing. From there they went to the new groves where young trees grew in the shade of the larger madre-de-cacao trees. They went to the groves of mature trees. These were the most beautiful trees that Red had ever seen. The trunks and largest branches were covered with delicate pink blossoms, and large pods of red, yellow, and orange.

Everywhere they went they saw men and boys working together.

Two things impressed Red this first day. The first was that not all boys everywhere have time for playing and for growing slowly into manhood. Some boys, as here, for instance, are born to be cacao workers. Their play time is work time in the clearings surrounded by cacao. Their school is the cacao groves. Their lives are part of the cacao finca.

The other thing that impressed him was that the chocolate that is bought in the store at Middlebury or at the Trading Post on the Reservation is the product of years of labor. It is the life of the chocolate laborer.

The finca was too large to be seen in a day or in many days.

Life took on a pattern, each day similar to the day before it, yet each day adding its bit to the design.

Red and his father left the hacienda early every morning. They rode to the clearing. They walked all day in the cacao groves, and nighttime found them back at the hacienda for dinner and for bed.

Red grew taller as he grew older. He had never had daily companionship with his father before. Now that he had it, he liked it. He saw his father in a new light. His father was like Gramp, he thought, not in appearance or in manner, but underneath. Underneath they both needed to understand, to know, to help other people.

Red asked questions. He had always asked questions. He always would. Questions were as much a part of him as the freckles across his nose. He asked questions of Dad and Señor Ramón. He asked questions of Papacito. Sometimes, caught off guard in the enthusiasm of some moment, he asked questions in halting, broken Spanish of the boys working so near him. They laughed at him. He did not know why they laughed, whether because of his poor Spanish or because they thought his questions funny. Perhaps they laughed because they did not know what else to do.

Gradually he could piece together the story of cacao. The people's legends said that the ancient gods had brought cacao seeds from the gardens of heaven to plant them in the gardens of man. The scientific name for cacao, Dad told him, meant "food of the gods."

Señor Ramón had a book in Spanish about cacao, and Red taught himself to read it. From it he learned that the Aztecs used the cacao beans for money. They were using it for barter at the time Cortes came to the Americas. They used it also for food. Mixing it with wine and honey or cinnamon and pepper, they used it as their ceremonial drink at their ancient sacrifices.

Reading the Spanish book helped Red in other ways besides learning the history of cacao. He found that it had taught him to listen in Spanish. Although his speech was still not good, he realized that he could understand.

He listened to the others talking and by listening he learned about the new groves and the old groves.

The seedling beds and the young trees and the mature trees belonged to the men. They planted and cultivated them. They weeded and sprayed them. They gathered the pod crop. They sold the beans to the banana company, which sent men to the clearing to buy them. They called these groves the "cash-crop groves" because their harvest was sold for the money that came into the settlement.

The old groves belonged to the women. These were called the "food groves." The cacao harvested from them was used for food by the people in the settlement. The women planted gardens of corn and okra, squash, beans, and tomatoes in these old groves.

Learning about the men-and-women division of property reminded Red of Hasteen, because the Navajos also had such a division.

Red longed for his friend. He longed for someone to talk to—not to listen to, but to talk to. Again he tried to talk with Juanito. His Spanish was better now. He was more at ease. But still there was little to talk about.

Juanito was not born to be a cacao worker. He was a hacienda employee. He helped Juan with the odd jobs. He helped Tio in the garden. He helped Lin in the kitchen. He helped Manuel in the dairy barn if there was real need for him there. He was not interested in the old groves or the new groves. The cacao world was a world apart from his.

Red understood this with a new understanding. The cacao world was not his world either. His world and Juanito's were much the same. Red knew this without being able to put it into words. I know we have something in common, he thought, using his grandfather's words, if only I could find what it is.

He tried making friends with the boys in the groves, knowing he would not succeed. He smiled at them as they passed him on the trails. They did not raise their eyes to see his offer of friendship. Sometimes he called to them. They did not raise their heads. Perhaps they did not hear him. He never knew.

Eating his lunch, wrapped in plantain leaves, Red squatted near where the men and boys were eating. The women brought the menfolk their lunches and served them. They sat in the shade, watching them eat, waiting for them to finish. Red wished he could tell them how like they were in this custom to the Pueblo Indians at home. He would have liked to tell them how the Indian women brought lunch to their men who worked in the fields and how they, too, sat nearby to watch them eat. But he did not tell them.

Red watched the little girls. Their work was to keep the parrots out of their mothers' garden plots. They screamed at the parrots. They called and shouted at them. They beat sticks together. The few who were fortunate enough to have tin pans beat on them with small, hard fists. They made a fearful racket. The parrots flew away, for a time, screeching and scolding.

Once in the midst of the noise, Red yelled too. He gave a loud "Yip-ee-a!" It felt wonderful to hear his own voice. But it terrified both the little girls and the parrots into silence. Red was embarrassed. He went away and never went back to watch the little girls again.

Once he went up to the women to offer to help them. But when he spoke to them some laughed at him, and others went on working and did not know or care if he was there.

Red watched his father to see if the people accepted him. The ones at the hacienda did. They were his servants. They were Mom's friends. But they were polite and gracious to Dad and also to himself, Red noticed.

Señor Ramón accepted Dad. He was Dad's assistant. The cacao workers accepted him with indifference. It was as if they knew that he was with them now, but that he would go away again. But Dad had his work. He had a mission to accomplish. The improvement of cacao for Dad was a living thing. It walked beside him. He thought of it by day and dreamed of it at night. His work was his companion.

Red walked the forest paths. They were cool and dark. Tree leaves made a roof overhead. Moss-thick grass made a carpet underfoot. There were orchids everywhere. They hung from the trees like sleeping butterflies. Cacao pods grew in clusters on the hard, green-brown tree trunks. Among the pods were star clusters of delicate rose-colored flowers with the center petal a perfect jaguar's claw. The ripe pods were golden yellow. He gathered armfuls of the pods for his mother. He gathered orchids for her, filling the jeep on the homeward trip each night.

Mom watched for his coming and came to the gateway to meet him, to welcome his flowers. But his offerings hurt her. She knew that he did not like them, not really. Gathering them was only something to do. Bringing them home to her was something to do with them. A candle to his loneliness, Mom thought.

Cacao harvest came. To Red the days became alike, running into each other like the winding forest trails, like the winding, rushing rivers. One day became like another, without name, without beginning or ending.

The men cut the ripe cacao pods from the trees. Red watched them. He thought the work must be very hard. The poles for cutting were three times as long as the men who used them. They seemed heavy. At one end a sharp knife was tied. This was for cutting the pod clusters from the trunk bark. The men worked with their heads thrust backward, their faces turned upward, slashing with the knives that were tied to their poles.

Red begged his father to get him a pole, to let him try using one. He knew he could do it, maybe not very well, but he could learn. He wanted to try. His father said no. He said this was not play but serious work. The men must be careful not to injure the tree bark nor the leaves. They must not injure the tiny flowerlets which in three or four months would become pods. Red knew he could do it if he had a chance, but such a chance was not given to him.

While the men cut the golden, melon-shaped pods from the tree trunks and branches, the women and children gathered them. Red watched them pile them into hills. When a hill of pods became waist high a man would squat beside it. With a slash of his sharp machete he would slit each thick pod husk lengthwise. Then the women would scoop out its juicy pulp and the pale, pink chocolate beans. The tool they used for this was made of a cow's rib. The women were quick and skillful. The beans were picked out carefully and the pod husks and pulp were thrown away.

The little girls in their white cotton dresses came drifting in like small, white clouds. On their heads they carried stacks of plantain leaves. They made beds of these leaves and put the rosy chocolate beans on them in straight rows. Watching them, Red thought of little girls in Middlebury putting their baby dolls to bed. Homesickness overcame him. He felt blind and sick. Then the world righted itself, and he saw these little girls as working children, not as small girls playing with toys.

The things they did were work—hard work—not play. It meant bending over, straightening up, sorting seeds, putting them down in rows on the plantain leaves. From misted morning until evening dusk they worked with a rest only at midday when the sun burned everything it touched with red-hot fingers.

After the beans had stayed in their leafy beds for several days, it was time to bring them to the clearing where the houses were. The beans that had been rosy pink were now a chocolate brown. The men carried them to the clearing in great sacks on their backs. The women carried them to the clearing in deep baskets on their heads. Red walked behind the procession with his father and Señor Ramón. He thought bitterly, What am I doing here? Watch. Watch. Watch. That's all I'm allowed to do.

At the clearing, drying platforms had been built to receive the beans. The platforms were made of split bamboo and covered with woven fiber mats. The beans were piled on these mats to dry. Each separate bean had to be turned over and over. They must be evenly dried. They must be turned and turned.

Red and Dad stayed late into the evenings now. They stayed to watch the boys dance on the beans. The boys' dancing bare feet polished the beans, shined them, glossed them, made them beautiful.

The air was filled with a rich chocolate smell.

At night the beans were covered so that rain would not wet them. Then they were sorted and sacked and weighed. Red offered to help with this. He could weigh. He could keep records. Reluctantly his father said no. This was too important for an outsider to manage. What if he made a mistake? What would happen if the workers thought he did? Red understood this. He agreed with his father. But even so, he was sick at heart.

He was tired of being an outsider. He was tired of being an onlooker. He wanted to be a doer, not a watcher. He wanted to be the boy in the midst of things, not one on the sidelines looking on.

This was almost September, the boy remembered. He had been here three months, or almost three. At home the boys would be getting ready for school. They would be in a new grade, trying out a new teacher. It would be like all Septembers, only he would not be there.

The club would start again. The boys would get their Scout badges for their summer's work. Only this year there would be no badge for him. He would not be getting the bird-watcher's badge.

The rain fell wetly against his face.

Red grew taller, thinner, quiet. The freckles paled across his nose. His mother fretted and his father worried. "We could send him back to the States," his father offered. "We could put him in boarding school."

Then a letter came from Gramp. It was in answer to Mother's worried one. "Give him time," Gramp's letter said. "He'll make it if you give him time."

"What shall we do?" Dad asked again. "I want him to be happy. Shall we send him home to school?"

Mother was quiet, thinking. She too wanted her Red to be a happy boy. Finally she answered, "Let's do as Gramp says. Let's give him time."

Chapter Nine

Red awakened slowly, his dream still with him. It was such a good dream, so real, so vivid, so alive. He thought he could keep it with him for a while by not coming awake too quickly, by keeping his eyes tightly closed and keeping his thoughts on the things that the dream brought with it.

Red listened, listened, willing himself to hear what the dream had brought him. Then it came again, a thin line of song, distinct in syllable, but faint in sound.

How well he knew that song! He had heard it every summer for as long as he could remember. "Wee-chee, chee, chee, chee-wee," the song of the northern warbler on the

Navajo Reservation. He tried to hum it, the warbler's song, remembering the warbler he had watched in his grandmother's lilac bush.

Red kept his eyes closed, looking backward in memory. Slowly he brought back the summer and the warblers he had seen nesting in the lilac. But there had been other warblers in other summers, too: the one swinging on a chokecherry branch over the stream where he and Hasteen had their campfire; the one singing his heart out in the early morning when he had been camping with Yellow-Shirt. They came back now in a line of warblers, in a line of summers— friendly, curious little fellows. They always seemed so interested in who you were and what you were doing and why you were there. Then, when they were satisfied, away they would flit into some gray-green thicket.

Red smiled, hearing the song again. It was a dream, of course. He knew he was not hearing a warbler's song, not really hearing it. What would the little beauty of the western wastelands be doing in the Costa Rican bush country?

The boy lay quiet, breathlessly listening to the clean, true, liquid sound pouring through the heavy morning.

He remembered the first warbler he had seen. He had been riding with Gramp and Hasteen on Navajo Mountain on a hot June day. They were eating lunch under a juniper tree, their horses standing nearby with heads drooping, reins dropped to the ground in the western way. He had been the first one to see the nest. There had been four eggs in it, blue-white eggs spotted and speckled with lavender and brown. Red remembered how gently they had moved away so the mother bird would come back to her nest. Even Gramp, big-shouldered, tall Gramp, had moved away without a sound.

Red opened his eyes. He heard the song again. He was awake now. His eyes were open. He was not asleep and dreaming. This was no dream! What he heard was real!

Red sat up in bed. His room was dark. He crept to the window. Cautiously he opened the shutters to watch the gray light sift in morning mist through the leafy trees. He watched and waited.

Sounds began to stir in the thick growth that bordered the hacienda clearing. Red turned. He tiptoed to the door, carrying his shoes, clutching his bathrobe about him. He passed his parents' bedroom door. The floor creaked beneath his stealthy steps. A stairstep creaked. He could hear his own heart beating. The great front door was barred with a heavy chain that rattled as he took it from its hooks. The door stuck and then groaned as he pushed against it.

At last he was out of the house. No one heard him. No one had seen him. No one had stopped him. No one knew that he had gone.

He was free to follow the song.

The boy drew a sigh of relief. Then he shuddered. The trees loomed skyward, dark, unfriendly, unfamiliar. Ropelike vines swung from the tree branches. Although there seemed to be no wind, no little morning breeze, the vines swung back and forth, back and forth, as if unseen hands were moving them. The vines clung blackly against the walls of the house behind him. They covered the verandas and framed the dark, closed shutters of the windows. Far in the brush the howler monkeys howled.

Red was afraid. Although he had not realized it before, he knew now that he had been afraid always of the thick, crowded tropical growth that pushed against the edges of the clearing. Perhaps that was why he had so wanted to explore its depths, to conquer it, to show it and himself that he was not afraid. Jaguars lived in the depths of the brush country, and tiger cats and pumas and wild pigs. Now he could almost see them crouching in the tree branches, creeping through the fern banks, waiting, watching for him to come.

"Wee-chee, chee, chee, chee-wee." Red stopped. He threw his bathrobe to one side. Already it was wet to his knees from the heavy dew. He put on his shoes. He said softly, "I'm coming, I'm coming to see if you are really true." His shoulders shook. His teeth chattered. He crept out into the opening, following the song.

He went across the clearing, past the servants' quarters and the springhouse and the barn and the fenced grass pasture. There were horses in the pasture, dark shadows in a gray-mist world. One of them nickered, and the sound brought him comfort. In all this unfamiliar world, this was a sound he knew—a sound from home.

The time of the heavy rains was over. There was only the heavy dew of night mist and the heavy shower at midday. The dry season was on its way to the brush country.

Red crossed the river that a few weeks ago had been a muddy torrent. Now it was clear in the early light, and the high, swinging bridge swung gently as he lightly crossed it. Quickly he reached the opposite bank.

Then the boy hesitated, waiting to hear the song that would mark his way.

It was lighter now, and he could see more clearly. He looked about. Almost underfoot he saw a hyacinth macaw. It did not move even when he bent over it. Then he saw that it was sorrowfully guarding its mate that had been killed. Hyacinth macaws mate for life. When one bird is killed the other bird guards it until it too dies and is free from its lonely vigil. "Poor fellow," Red said softly, looking down at the drooping, brilliantly colored bird. "Poor fellow," he repeated, wishing there were some way he could help it.

In the thicket beside him something moved, then swung up and was lost in the treetops. Peering upward he saw a monkey swinging in the branches and peering down at him.

Red laughed. Then he heard the warbler's song again and started forward to follow its sound. It led straight into the bushes. He had never gone into the overgrown, tangled growth. He knew he should not go, and looked around for some kind of trail. There was no trail.

He heard the song again. Blindly he pushed through the bushes. Thorns scratched him. Branches slapped him. The vines were tangled and matted. He heard, or thought he heard, a swishing movement underfoot, and his heart caught in his throat.

But almost at once he was through the thicket. A natural, parklike clearing lay before him. The mist now was treetop high, rising slowly in swelling billows. The grass under his feet was thick and spongy and dotted with star flowers unfolding their petals.

The bird song came again, then stopped in mid-tone. A boy was whistling it. Red went closer. It was Juanito, who jumped up quickly to his feet. Red, who thought he could speak no Spanish, spoke Spanish now, spoke it quickly, clearly in rising excitement. "That's the warbler's song, isn't it? I know it is. How did you learn it? What do you know about a warbler and his song?"

Juanito was silent. He stood looking at Red in wordless surprise.

"Where did you learn the song?" Red asked again. "How do you know about my birds?"

"Your birds?" Juanito asked, also in Spanish, neither boy realizing that at last the language gap was bridged. Their surprise lay in what the other boy was saying, not in the language he was using. "Your birds?" Juanito asked again.

Red hesitated. "No," he said, "not my birds. They are wild birds. But I know them so well. I never could get their song just right. How did you learn it?"

"I know them, too," Juanito said simply. "That's why I'm here today. Today is when the warblers come."

Red's face was white. "You don't mean—you can't mean our birds come way down here!"

Juanito nodded, but he did not speak.

After a moment Red said wonderingly, "You mean they migrate here. I always knew," he added slowly, "about migration. But it was just a word I used, I guess, without thinking much about it. I guess I never realized what it meant."

"The first flock," Juanito told him, "comes today. They are never late."

Red could not believe what he was hearing. He could not believe that the little yellow fellows of the Navajo country could come to Costa Rica. He could not believe that probably, just probably, some bird he had seen at home he would see again today. What if the yellow babies of early summer he had seen hatched, he had watched learn to fly, would come here today? It could be so, it could happen. He would never know, but it could be true. It could be possible.

Suddenly his eyes were filled with tears. He felt them on his face. He tasted them in his mouth. He fought a sob that choked his throat. Quickly Red turned his back, ashamed to face Juanito.

Surprise pushed the tears away. "Look," he called over his shoulder to Juanito. "Look! There's Lin and Quaco."

Juanito did not answer. He had known they were there. At last he said, "They are here to watch for the birds. We come to welcome them. We like them very much. Do you?"

"I love them," Red said slowly.

The mist had melted. The sun's bright rays were deepening the sky's early-morning blue. There was a moment of quiet, of expectancy, of waiting.

Over the treetops was a whir of wings. Against the sky was a melody of song. The warblers were coming.

They poured over the treetops in a swelling wave, a liquid flow of color. They rained down from the heavens, hundreds and hundreds and hundreds of sun-colored birds. They covered the trees and the bushes with splashes of yellow. They dotted the flower-strewn grass with spots of gold.

Still more came. The air was thick with the soft whir of wings. "There are thousands," Red whispered. "Look. They are young birds. Every one of them."

"The young ones come first," Lin said quietly. "In a week or two the old ones will come."

"It's a miracle," Red said.

Lin smiled. "It is the mystery of migration. It is the great mystery of nature. It is the power of God."

"The power of God," Red repeated. "Well, everything is through God's power. But what is it besides God that makes birds migrate?" Then quickly, answering his own question, "It's food, maybe. You know, plants and insects being scarce in fall must make them want to leave."

Quaco answered slowly. "That might be. Food might call them here. Nesting might call them north again."

Lin shook his head. "That is not what I am talking about. I am talking about the mystery of migration. Warblers come here to this exact spot year after year. They return to the north to the same nesting place year after year. They come at the same time of year. They must leave at a certain time in order to arrive here at a certain time. How do they know when to go? How do they have such a sense of time?"

Red would have interrupted, but Lin raised his hand for silence, and continued speaking. "Take these birds here. They are young birds. This has been their first flight. How did they know that this is where the warblers come? How could they find their way across a trackless ocean, across a trackless sky? Perhaps the pull of the sun, you say? These birds fly by night and feed and rest by day. What guides them is the power of God."

Red was speechless with amazement, not so much from what Lin had been saying, but from the way he said it. Where was the man who laughed when he talked, and spoke in jerky phrases? This man spoke as Yellow-Shirt would have spoken. He spoke as a man of wisdom. What was it that had changed him so?

Then Red realized that he himself had been speaking in Spanish. He had no trouble. Words had poured from his heart. Now that he had something to talk about he found that he could talk.

What his grandfather had said came back to him in broken phrases, but the meaning was there. "The bonds that tie us together are what we like together, are what we share." Gramp had called them common interests, common values. I understand him now, Red thought. He looked at

Quaco, Lin, and Juanito. They were not different. They were not strangers. They were his friends.

The man and the boys were silent. They gazed at the living, beating, fluttering yellow world around them. They listened to a thousand birds sing the joyous "wee-chee" song.

Chapter Ten

Everyone helped plan for the adventure. Red, Juanito, and Lin were the ones who were going on the journey, but everyone helped plan for it. Everyone gave advice. No one listened. The whole hacienda was filled with activity and noise and laughter. This was no everyday journey that anyone could take. This was a once-in-a-lifetime adventure. It was worth waiting for and planning for.

Red, Juanito and Lin were to visit the Bird Woman's place in the heart of the jungle lowlands. No roads led to it. No trails led out. It was a place unto itself, isolated, complete, unheard of by the rest of the world. Lin knew of it, but then Lin had hidden wisdom and secret knowledge that only the few who had the key to his heart would ever learn.

Lin knew the Bird Woman's place and he knew the Bird Woman herself. She was an Indian, old, old, having lived more years than she could count. There were few Indians in Costa Rica—few that were left. These few lived deep in the jungle interior, hidden from settlements, from towns, from civilization, from all other kinds of people. They had re-treated to the safe heart of the untamed forests when white men discovered their world. There they were living today as they had lived thousands of years ago, untouched by time or by changes in history.

The Bird Woman headed these Indians. She was the oldest one. She was the one most revered by her people. Few out-siders had heard of her, but the few who had whispered about her. These whispered words were passed from ear to ear, a single, slender thread around the world.

The birds of the world knew her, the whispers said. They came by the tens of thousands to visit her. Some stayed for many months, and others winged their way briefly over the place where the old Indian lived.

The whispers said many other things. They said the old Bird Woman held the fly-ways of the world in the magic of her hands, and the song-ways of the world in the magic of her heart. Lin knew these things he whispered to Juanito and to Red. To Mother and Father he said brightly, "A good place to take them, a beautiful place." He told them no more than that.

Even Dad was excited about the trip. He kept wishing that he could go. In all the hacienda, Mom was the only one not pleased. She worried. She was afraid. She said she did not like the thought of Red's going on such a dangerous journey.

Juanito's eyes were big and tragic. "What if she does not let you go?" he whispered to Red.

"Mom," Red said, "there's no danger. It's just an old jungle. Please let me go."

"All friends there," Lin added, chuckling and beaming.

Red looked at him sharply and quickly looked away again. Lin was using his everyday speech now and not the kind he had used when he talked to him on the morning of the miracle. To himself that was the name the boy had given to the morning when the birds had come. Their coming had been a miracle in itself. But with their coming another miracle had happened. The birds had brought on wings of gladness, a bond of understanding and acceptance that tied an old man and three boys together in a union of spirit that would last them through the years to come.

Red was happy. He could not remember a time when he had been so completely happy. Every day was filled with things to do, now that he had someone who shared their doing.

The boy brought his gaze back to his mother's face. She had not, he decided, made up her mind, but she was ready to make it up. Once it was made up, Red knew, there would be no changing her.

Juanito also looked at his friend's mother. He said nothing, but his dark eyes begged her to say that Red could go.

Red took a deep breath. Perhaps if he told her a little something about the trip, not about the Bird Woman, of course . . . The Bird Woman and her power were not to be talked about in casual conversation. But he could tell his mother about a gathering place for migratory birds. That would be all right. That was common knowledge and not a whispered secret.

He took a deep breath again. "It will be educational," he told his mother earnestly. "Lin says that now there will be more birds in that part of Costa Rica than anywhere else on earth. Maybe I'll get to see all kinds of birds, even some from as far away as the Arctic Circle."

Finally Dad said, "I'll send Quaco with them." Red looked quickly at Quaco. Did Quaco know about the Bird Woman? He looked deep into Quaco's eyes. Yes, he knew, Red decided. Quaco was one of the secret circle.

"I'll send Quaco with them," Dad repeated. "He will be one more person to take care of your precious child."

Mom's eyes snapped. "What do you mean, 'take care of'?" she demanded. "Red needs no one to take care of him. He can take care of himself. Of course he can go." Mom looked around as if she expected someone to say Red could not go.

No one spoke. No one moved. There were no triumphant looks exchanged, no joyful glances. It was better, safer, too, to prepare to go, quietly and quickly.

Dad asked Quaco if he would like to go on the jungle journey, and Quaco answered that he would be the first one ready.

So it had been decided. The trip became a reality.

Lin explained the route carefully. To get to the place would take three days. First they would fly to a Spanish settlement that Lin knew about, which lay on the edge of the jungle. It would be a day's ride from there to a certain river landing. "What river landing?" Mom asked. "No name, just there," Lin answered. Then the party would go to the place by dugout canoe, as the Indians' only outlet to the sea was by river.

The old Chinese continued with his explanation. He had everything planned, in detail and with care. The banana company would fly them to Isabella, the Spanish settlement at the jungle's edge. The company would use one of its small planes, which could carry five besides the pilot. They were lending hammocks and mosquito netting for sleeping at night, as the trip would take as least nine days.

"When can we start?" Red was impatient. "When can we start? I can be ready by morning."

Lin chuckled. "Not tomorrow. No." He laughed, shaking his head at the anxious boy. "Two weeks. Ready in two weeks."

"Two weeks!" Red repeated in disbelief. "Why will it take so long to get ready?"

"Much to do," Lin answered, "much to do. Have to send word."

It was Mom's turn to ask a question. "Send word? By whom?"

"By those who know." Surprisingly it was Quaco who gave this answer.

Mom shook her head. She felt bewildered, as if there were things about this trip she did not know.

The days passed swiftly. The company doctor came from Limón to give the boys shots against jungle sickness and insect bites and stings. He gave them K-rations for their food supply and tablets to purify the drinking water.

Mom kept asking questions. "What happens when you get to this Spanish settlement? Where will you stay at night?"

"Hotel there," Lin answered.

"How will you get to the Indian settlement? The one you call the place."

Lin chuckled. "Mule-back—trail," he answered. "Dugout —river."

Suddenly Dad seemed worried also. He checked the supplies over and over and added extra items. He added a hammock and mosquito net. He added to the K-rations. "But why?" Red asked, "why?"

"You might need extra things," Dad insisted.

Red fretted. "We have what we need. Why extra things?"

"You might need them," Dad insisted.

Only a week was left—a week Red knew that would seem to be a whole year long.

Dad decided to go to Limón. He took Quaco with him to drive the jeep. He would not say why he was going. He would give no explanation to anyone, saying only, "Look for me to be back tomorrow night."

Red and Juanito spent both days at the warblers' clearing. Since their last visit the old birds had joined the younger ones. The boys spent hours watching the flitting, floating, soaring bits of feathered sunshine. They talked little. It was satisfying enough just to sit silently, watching the birds.

On the second evening Dad came home. Red was sitting on the steps watching for him. He saw the jeep coming— a tiny, moving speck in a world of green. The jeep came nearer, nearer.

Red stood up. There were more people in the jeep than Quaco and Dad. There were two more people. It wasn't— it couldn't be. It was! It was! Red shouted, "Mom! Mom! It's Gramp and Hasteen. They've come with Dad!"

The jeep stopped. Everyone crowded around it. Everyone talked at the same time. Gramp and Hasteen stood looking at Red. They were laughing, holding out their hands to him.

Red did not wait to see their hands, did not wait to shake them. He hugged them both and sobbed. He was so glad that he forgot to be ashamed to cry.

"Surprise for you, Redhead," Gramp shouted. "Heard from your mother that you fitted in here like the place had been built for you. Hasteen and I decided to come see for ourselves how well you made it."

"He made it," Dad said, smiling at his son. It was the first time Dad had used Gramp's words of praise. Red knew he meant them. He stood with pride.

"What have you and your dad been doing?" Gramp asked.

Red grinned at his father. "Dad and I've been making bridges," he answered teasingly. "Dad made his of chocolate and mine is made of feathers." Mom looked startled at such a peculiar answer, but she was pleased. A boy and his father should be good friends enough to have secret jokes between them, she thought.

Gramp looked over his glasses at his redheaded grandson. "Feathers?" he asked.

"Birds," Hasteen said. They laughed. They seemed to understand the meaning beneath the words.

By this time they had gone into the house. Lin and Tio, Juan and Juanito, Carmencita and Marita came forward to greet them. They were delighted that visitors had come. The hacienda had been too quiet. The servants missed the old days when the hacienda owner and his family had been at home. Since they had gone there had been no gay hacienda parties lasting a week, no houseful of visiting kinfolk, no dances, no fiestas, no *serenadas*. The North Americans had been too quiet.

"The Old One will be good to have around," Tio said in Spanish. "He brings laughter with him."

Gramp made a little bow. "I am *simpatico*," he told them gravely.

"The Old One speaks the Spanish," Tio murmured in amazement.

Everyone laughed. Suddenly they felt friendly toward each other. Gramp was simpatico.

Quaco brought in the luggage, suitcases, boxes, and bundles. "Staying three weeks," Gramp explained. "Then Hasteen has to be back at school."

Talk went on endlessly from early morning until almost early morning again. Gramp asked about the trip that was being planned. "Hasteen is going with us," Red told him. "That's why Dad put in all those extra things. He knew Hasteen was coming and that, of course, he would go with us."

Red was quiet for a time. His freckles popped out across his nose as they always did when he was deeply moved. At last he offered, "Go in my place, Gramp. I want you to go."

Gramp looked alarmed. "I don't want to go, Redhead. I want to keep my feet on the ground for a week or two." Then, seeing Red's disbelief, he added, "Tell you what, when you come back we'll go see a volcano. I've always wanted to see a volcano."

"We'll go to Irazu." Red was enthusiastic. "Lin says that from the top of Irazu you can see the Atlantic Ocean thirty-five miles away and the Pacific Ocean sixty miles away. The land is only that wide there from ocean to ocean. Just think, Gramp, the same distance as from the Trading Post to Gallup."

Gramp was impressed. "Learning geography at first hand," he said.

Red grinned up at the tall old man. "I'm learning more than geography. You'll see some of it this morning. We have a bird surprise for you."

Chapter Eleven

Juanito and Red took Gramp and Hasteen to see the warblers. Red led the way, importantly, but secretly remembering his terror on his first dawn trip to the clearing. There still was danger—danger from tripping in the tangled vines, danger from snake bite, and a possible danger, though not a likely one, from a prowling puma.

Red was impatient to get to the clearing, but he made himself walk slowly. He wanted Gramp and Hasteen to get the full flavor of the misty dawn, the feel of heat laying its blanket softly over the dew-jeweled world. He wanted them to smell each smell, to hear each rustle in the fern banks and each call in the treetops. Although the trail was now known to him—he had been over it so often—it still held thrill, suspense, promise of a special something.

Juanito walked at the end of the line, watching the ones in front of him with alert, protective eyes. No one spoke as they walked stealthily along. It was not a time for speaking. Not one of them would have wanted, or have dared, to break the secret-filled hush of a misty dawn in the bush country.

At last they reached the clearing and stood speechless at the beauty before them. The old birds were with the young birds now.

At last Gramp broke the silence. "To think," he said hoarsely, "that any one of these little fellows might have been hatched out in your grandmother's lilac bush."

Red smiled in delight. "I think that, too, every time I come here. They are so little to find the way. They are such little things to—to sort of tie the world together. You know—like a thin, strong cord tying countries and people together." Red laughed in embarrassment, hoping they would understand what he was trying so hard to say.

Juanito said something in Spanish, but so lightly, so quickly, that Red could not translate it.

"Yellow-Shirt always said the summer yellow birds had a special meaning for you." Hasteen spoke quietly, gazing at the soaring birds among the trees.

"He did say that," Red said in surprise. "But how did you remember it? I had forgotten."

"I've been trained to remember the words that Yellow-Shirt speaks," Hasteen answered.

Red nodded, remembering Hasteen's letter that had said

someday he would have to take the old medicine man's place. How long ago that seemed. How far away that life seemed to be. Middlebury was like a dream, the Trading Post a dear, remembered place.

The four sat in companionable silence until the first spatter of afternoon rain. Then they reluctantly turned their backs on the clearing and faced the homeward trail.

Red walked closely behind his Indian friend. There were things he needed to say to him.

Red had asked Lin if he could tell Hasteen about the Bird Woman. Lin had answered gravely. He never chuckled when he was talking alone with the boys. Words then were serious and to be pondered. "If you are certain," Lin had replied, "that this boy is one to treasure such knowledge, tell him."

"I am certain," Red said with conviction.

Now the opportunity had come to tell Hasteen those whispered words which had been told to him. "You are going with us to the place," he began cautiously. "This place where we are going—" he spoke very low, but very clearly. It was necessary that Hasteen understand the importance of what he was hearing. "This place—" he began again, but Hasteen interrupted him.

"I know the place," Hasteen said, barely opening his lips. "I know about the Bird Woman. I have heard of her." Then, feeling Red's amazement, he said, simply, "Have you forgotten? I too am Indian."

The boys walked on in silence, each busy with his own thoughts. Red was thinking, So he knew all the time. He knows so many things that I will never know, not book things that all can know who can read, but knowledge passed on by words from mouth to mouth.

After a while he said, "Hasteen, I want you to know that now I appreciate all the things you have given me."

Hasteen turned his head in surprise.

Red hastened to explain. "I don't mean things you can see and touch. I mean things like language. You learned my language so we could talk together. I didn't realize what that meant before, but now I do. Now that I am trying so hard to say all that I want to say in Spanish."

Hasteen nodded. "Language is a bridge. Someone has to make it and to cross it." Then, imitating Gramp's hearty voice, he said, "I made it."

Both boys laughed. Red felt comfortable and natural and hungry. He said to Juanito, "When we get to the barns, these two foreigners can come on alone. I'll race you to the hacienda steps."

When they arrived at the hacienda, the company doctor was there, waiting to give Hasteen his shots for the jungle trip. "Are there many more," he asked, "who are making this unnecessary journey?" He felt cross. It had taken him two days to get to the hacienda this second time. Why let these boys go off into the jungle? he wondered. Why not keep them at the hacienda where they belonged?

At last the morning of departure came. Everyone and everything was packed and ready to go.

They crowded into the jeep and the jeep truck to ride to the banana company's landing field. Mom went with them, to say a last good-by, to speed them on their way, to give last-minute instructions. Mom had not been away from the hacienda since she had arrived so many months ago. She felt as if she were taking a trip to the moon. "You and I," Gramp whispered to her, "are going into San José to see the sights." Mom liked that. She longed to see a city street again.

Red was so happy that he felt light-headed, giddy. He was so happy that a lump kept coming in his throat. He had to look straight ahead. He dared not look around at anyone. I never knew before, he thought in silent wonder, that happiness can hurt as much as sorrow can.

The sun-warmed morning was green and gold. The air was spicy with cinnamon and sweet with vanilla smells. Parrots darted through the trees like broken bits of sunshine. Butterflies swarmed among the bushes like flowers with petaled wings.

Hasteen said in rapture, "What a beautiful country! In only a year or so from now you will have to leave it forever."

"Not me. Not forever," Red told him. "I'm coming back someday."

"I'll come with you," Hasteen promised.

"But what if you take Yellow-Shirt's place?"

Hasteen spoke slowly. "If I take Yellow-Shirt's place with our people . . ." Then quickly Hasteen corrected himself. "When I take his place I will bring to our people the wisdom of the old, but—" Hasteen stopped. He looked very Indian and very like old Yellow-Shirt. His voice, when he continued, was like Yellow-Shirt's voice. "But I will add color to the ancient design by also bringing to the people a knowledge of the new."

Dad called to the boys to help Quaco load their supplies. The landing place was a scene of efficiency and haste. There were other small planes there besides the one the boys would take. Their plane was warming up, getting ready to take off.

The pilot hailed Red. "Hey, Redhead, aren't you too young to go exploring?"

Red answered stiffly, "I've done lots of exploring in the Navajo country and I'm an old hand at flying, too. I've been in the air three times."

The pilot laughed.

Mom said in an undertone to Dad, "I had not realized how tall Red has become."

"Red's growing up," Dad told her proudly.

"But twelve is so young," Mom answered wistfully.

"Twelve is a good beginning," Dad answered.

Cargo and passengers were loaded quickly, and quick good-bys were said. Inside all was order and compactness. On one side were two double seats facing each other. The boys sat here. On the other side was the space reserved for cargo and a single seat for Lin.

A landing-field attendant closed the door. He dragged the steps away. Last good-bys were waved. The plane took off.

Almost immediately they were over the jungle. The pilot flew low, skimming the tops of the tallest trees so the boys could see the canopy of living green beneath them. The rounded treetops made a sea of rolling green. Their branches touched and interlaced. Through them, weaving in and out, braiding them, twisting and tying them together, were thick, heavy vine ropes. "Lianas," Quaco called the vine ropes and added, "The canopy is so thick nothing can filter through it except fine raindrops and twisted sunrays."

In about two hours they reached the settlement of Isabella, where the plane would leave them. The pilot banked and circled and landed on a flat grassy place as gracefully as a bird alighting at a desert water hole.

The boys helped Quaco unload their supplies. "Okay,

Redhead," the pilot shouted in farewell. "Be back in seven days to pick you up. Be sure you're here waiting for me or you'll have to walk back home."

The plane took off from the clearing as lightly as it had landed. In seconds it had disappeared above the canopy of green.

The boys stood where the plane had left them. Their feet sank deeply into the matted grass.

The first lap of the journey had been accomplished.

Chapter Twelve

The settlement of Isabella had few people—twenty, twenty-five perhaps. All of them gathered around to watch the plane come in, discharge its passengers, and take flight again.

The people knew Lin. They greeted him with respect. They were puzzled by the other passengers and stared at them in frank curiosity.

Red stared back at them with interest as great as theirs. These people were not Indian. They were Latin. He could tell by their features and their walk. But they did not look like the people he had seen in San José or the few Costa Ricans who lived at the hacienda. These people were more withdrawn, more reserved. "They have a kind of ancient-Bible-times look," Red said to Hasteen in English.

Red looked around. Lin was talking Spanish with the people and Quaco stood beside him, listening. Hasteen and Juanito had finished loading the supplies into an oxcart that had been waiting for them. Red went over to pat the patient oxen, to look into their great sad eyes. He wished he could talk with them.

When the loading was finished, everyone turned toward the settlement. One of the men gave Red a long, sharp-pointed pole and showed him how to direct the oxen by gently prodding their heavy, muscled necks.

There were about a dozen houses in the settlement. Even in the movies in Middlebury Red had never seen their like before. They were walled with bamboo and thatched with plantain leaves. They were not propped up on stilts as at the cacao finca, but built solidly on the grassy ground. The roofs were high, so steeply sloping, so overhanging that they made the houses look like tall, steep tents.

The houses were not built in rows as at the finca, nor around a plaza like Pueblo houses at home, nor in clusters like Navajo hogans. They were placed anywhere their builders fancied. There were no streets, but narrow, grass-lined pathways wound in and out among the buildings.

The oxen, the people, Lin, and the boys stopped before the hotel. Red, remembering the elegance of the one in San José, grinned in delight at this one which was a large, three-walled bamboo structure with an open front. There were no windows, no doors, no lights, no floors, no proprietor. There was no furniture. There were pegs on which to hang the hammocks—nothing more. "Mom would love this," Red whispered to Hasteen.

The people helped unload the luggage and hang the hammocks on the pegs and drape the mosquito nets over them. Then they wandered away, their curiosity satisfied. These were Lin's friends. He was taking them somewhere.

The boys were hungry. "All right," Lin told them. "We go to a friend now. We eat with him." He took them to the store, a building like the houses. It was small, jumbled, crowded with many kinds of things—dried fish in piles, rice in open baskets, seashells, gourds, baskets and baskets of dried herbs and candle bunches tied together and hanging in lines from wall to wall. The owner, Lin's friend, was a chubby, friendly, wrinkled old Chinese.

"What do you know! A Chinese here! How did he get here?" Red asked Quaco.

Quaco shrugged. "Orientals are everywhere. They are like birds, I think. They migrate."

The boys spent the afternoon wandering around, looking at everything. The people were friendly. They spoke to the boys in Spanish. Red's answers were hesitant. With strangers he still had little confidence in his Spanish, but Hasteen spoke with ease. "He learned to cross the language bridge early," Red thought sadly. "I wish we had spoken a dozen different languages at home."

Soon Lin found them to call them back to the store to eat dried fish, fried rice, and a delicious stew that looked and tasted like chicken. "Don't eat it if you don't want to," Quaco whispered. "I think it's monkey stew."

Night came to the settlement. The trees seemed to grow taller, darker, and to move in closer. Above the settlement a spot of sky could be seen, brooding over the people, lighting their clearing with low-hanging tropical stars. Children laughed. Fireflies danced in the soft, warm, perfume-thickened dusk. Somewhere someone strummed a guitar.

Somewhere someone sang a Spanish lullaby, coaxing a baby to sleep.

The boys sat in front of the lonely hotel. Lin was not with them. He was at the store, visiting his friend.

"Funny thing," Red observed. "This place is full of things —trees and plants and flowers, birds and insects and animals and even people nearby. Yet it seems lonelier than the Navajo country, where there is nothing but red rocks and sand. More primitive here, maybe," he added.

Hasteen laughed. "More primitive than the Fire Dance on the Navajo?"

Red joined his laughter. "Primitive is not the word to use, I guess," he said. "But it seems so strange." He was quiet for a while; then he said, half to himself, "I've come a long way."

"It's been a long journey," Juanito agreed, "many miles."

Suddenly, quietly, a strange man came out of the shadows and sat beside the boys. He was an old man with matted, long, white hair and piercing blue eyes. Red leaned closer in the fading light to see if it was true that this old man's eyes were blue. They were blue, a peculiar, glinting blue. The old man's trousers were in rags, tattered and dirty, shin-length and tied at the belt with a piece of rope. He wore no other clothing. His feet were bare.

The stranger spoke to them. Softly, tonelessly, he mumbled, mostly in English with a Spanish phrase thrown in from time to time. "You come from far places. Five people. Four races. But you come as friends. Your friendship is not built upon sand, but upon rock. It will last. It will endure, because it has a purpose. I know the secret of your mission. I, the outcast, the pauper, the forgotten one, I know it, too. It is not the secret of kings or of beggars. It is the secret of those who are bound together by the ropes of the wild birds' song."

The boys were startled, hushed, afraid. The stranger did not look at them. It was as if they were not there, as if he were not there, only a voice droning on and on, rising, falling like the wind in the trees.

Lin came back. He spoke sharply to the stranger. The old man walked away, back into the shadows out of which he had come. Red watched him go and felt tears sting his eyes. The old man seemed so alone, so lost, and yet he knew the secret. Red took a step after him, but stopped. What could he say? What could he offer to a wanderer who knew only the kinship of the wild birds' song?

Lin spoke sharply, bringing Red back into the circle of known things again. "Sleep now," Lin said crossly. "Morning comes too early."

Red grinned. The old Chinese was displeased with them. He had shut them out of his inner circle of cultured speech. He spoke to them now as outsiders, letting them know without words that their questions about the stranger would go unanswered. Lin left them shortly to sit hunched in the starlighted shadow of the bamboo wall.

Quaco showed them how to hang their bark hammocks and how to lie crossways in them, wrapping the folds about them to keep their bodies tight in the hammock, safe from falling. After each boy was in and wrapped in the hammock, Quaco hung the mosquito nets above them, letting the ends cling closely to the hammock sides. Red giggled. "I feel like a bride in all this veiling," he said.

The jungle trees were full of noises. The night hunters stole along their narrow trails. Red shivered, although the night was warm.

Out of the darkness Quaco whispered, "The stranger is an Englishman."

"He is an educated man. I heard him quoting Shake-speare," Hasteen said, low-voiced so Lin would not hear.

"Perhaps he belongs to some strange brotherhood and wanders around the world," Juanito said, forgetting in his excitement to speak softly.

Quaco spoke again. "No. I think he is an exiled English lord."

"Maybe a spy," Hasteen ventured.

Red said nothing. He was still held in awe at the things the stranger had said. Whatever he was, he was one of the secret circle whose heart spoke with the wild birds.

Lin spoke crossly. "No spy. No English lord. No philos-opher. Smuggler. Hiding here twenty years. I know. Sleep now. Morning comes too early."

But only Quaco slept, snoring gently. Night howlers howled. Night hunters moaned. Bark hammocks swished as restless boys tried to sleep.

Red was not sleepy; neither was he restless. He lay quietly, his blue eyes looked out into the velvet tropical night.

Morning did come too early, as Lin had warned. Red, half awake when he heard Lin calling, got tangled in his ham-mock and his mosquito net and sprawled full-length on the grassy ground of the hotel floor.

Food this morning was much the same as yesterday— fried rice, fried fish, bits of hard-fried pork, and mangoes to finish the meal.

When they had eaten, the mules were waiting, one for each of them, one for Lin's friend who would go with them, and a pack mule with the hammocks and mosquito nets.

Hasteen grumbled to Red, "I never saw such saddles as

they have in this country. Those English saddles they had at the hacienda were like postage stamps, and these . . . It's like trying to ride on a table top!"

Red laughed, but he said in quick defense, "These are typical Costa Rican saddles."

Hasteen still grumbled. "I think these are tied to the mule's ears and tails. Give me a western saddle any time, or better yet, ride bareback."

The trees rose straight and tall around them, each pushing upward to add its rounded top to the canopy that roofed the jungle world. There were no low tree branches and there was no undergrowth. Plants and trees alike grew tall, tall, taller, reaching upward to the sunlight.

This morning the jungle steamed. Heat rose upward from the trail. It pressed downward from above. Quaco, who was leading, reined his mule and pointed silently to the side of the trail. There, drinking at a forest pool, was a long-nosed tapir that disappeared into the forest gloom almost as quickly as they saw him.

Spider monkeys were everywhere, swinging on the vine ropes, jumping through space as lightly as if they were borne on wings. Hasteen, who was a perfect horseman, nearly fell from his mule when he caught a glimpse of an ugly-old-man face in a pointed beard peering down at him through a liana loop. "That is a howler monkey," Quaco called. "He is the one, perhaps, that sent shivers down your spine last night."

The mules kept up a brisk walk, the same pace always, neither quickening nor slacking. The hours passed by, each hour bringing them into darker, damper, stiller gloom.

By noon they had reached the river—a broad, muddy,

swift-flowing, violent stream—where they dismounted. Here Lin's friend left them, tying the string of mules, tails to bridles, and driving them back along the trail again. He called as he left, "I'll be back in four days. Be waiting."

The boys stood hunched together, feeling the lonely majesty of the great virgin forest. They did not talk. They were too excited, too awed for an escape through words.

Only Quaco and Lin took their surroundings for granted. They walked to the river's edge, looking upstream for the dugouts of the Indians.

The forest was still in the deathlike stillness of midday; only the heat moved in unseen waves. Quaco and Lin came back. Quaco made a stick-circle fire of a handful of dead branches he had picked at the river edge. He arranged the sticks like spokes in a wheel. There was fire enough only to boil water for tea. Food consisted of crackers, soggy and damp, fried rice cakes, dried fish, and fruit. The boys were hungry. They ate with enjoyment.

Suddenly a string of dugouts appeared, gliding noiselessly to the landing. The Indians poling them were short, compact, strong-looking men. They wore little clothing, and their bodies were rich mahogany color—much darker than Hasteen's, Red thought, looking at his friend.

The Indians greeted Lin as if they knew him. There were friendship, respect, and dignity in their greeting. They also spoke quietly with Quaco. They know him, too, Red thought. Perhaps not as well as they know Lin, but he is no stranger here.

"Lin's talking to them in their own language," Hasteen said. "Isn't it amazing how many languages he can speak?"

The Indians looked at each boy appraisingly, then turned

away. They spoke together for a time, then turned again to Hasteen. They spoke to him gravely and at length.

"They know you are Indian also," Lin explained. "Speak to them in your Indian tongue."

Hasteen did, and he thought that now and then they understood a word or two. But when they answered him he could not understand. "Might as well be Greek," he said sadly.

The Indians squatted around the fire, talking with Lin and Quaco and sharing with the boys the food they had brought. They had woven bags of dried meat not unlike jerky, the dried deer meat of the Navajos, and strange dried berries and fruits.

The afternoon was a short one, shadows falling early, followed almost immediately by velvet night.

The boys talked little, content to listen, although they understood not a word that was said. Presently one of the Indians began to sing. When he had finished another one sang, and then another, going clockwise around the circle. Lin's song was a high falsetto, sounding a little like a lone Navajo singing his flock to rest. Quaco sang a Jamaican lullaby. Then it was Hasteen's turn. "Sing the Bluebird Song," Red urged him. "If you sing it I can help you."

"Ah, ho, ho, ho, ho," Hasteen sang,
"Ee, hee, hee, hee yah, hee yah."

As the first words soared into the treetops the Indian visitors joined the singing. The words, rhythm, the beat, the song were the same.

"Nah, hah, yah," they sang,
"Hah, nah, yah."

Hasteen and Red sang clearly, and the Indians' soft clapping, soft pounding, soft syllables joined in perfectly. After a while the others joined them. Red-skinned, black, yellow, white-skinned people sang the Bluebird Song together.

Lin spoke gently into the hush that followed. "Sleep well, my little friends. Tomorrow will be long and difficult."

Tonight there were no restless, sleepless boys. Tonight there was only quiet sleeping. On the forest edge by an unknown river strange men wakened to listen, to guard and hold the sleeping boys.

Morning came breathless, hot and steaming, thickly shrouded in river mist. The dugouts were loaded with hammocks and nets and passengers. The last lap of the long journey lay before them.

Red was afraid. He could not remember ever being so afraid. He was afraid of the river. It looked so violent and mysterious. He was afraid of the dugout. He thought it looked too small for such a wide, big river. He sat flat on the bottom, gritting his teeth, willing himself not to shake with fear. His bright red hair stood stiffly upright. His freckles marched across his nose. His blue eyes were very blue. The Indians were interested. They had never seen a redheaded, blue-eyed child before. His red hair pleased them. His white skin amazed them. As for his blue eyes, they feared them a little. "His eyes are like the wanderer's," they said, "like the old one of Isabella who hides from the world, but brings to us his lonely heart."

The river swirled and foamed, lashing madly against the sides of the canoe. Red looked out at the river. He looked at the Indian in front of him, standing upright, poling swiftly. Jagged rocks thrust upward through the rushing water, the dugouts barely, although skillfully, missing them. Red felt sick. Stealing a look at Hasteen at the other end of the dugout, he saw that the young Indian was as afraid and as sick as he was. Somehow this comforted him. It made him feel better. It made the adventure more bearable.

The river was walled in green, broken by inlets almost hidden by vines. Sometimes a strange canoe would dart out from an inlet and pass them like a silver streak. The river sides were thick with alligators sunning lazily on sun-warmed, water-soaked logs.

The hours moved slowly. Red's fear left him, and gradually so did the sickness that had accompanied it. By and by he learned to accept the rhythm of the river. Little by little he began to like what he saw, to feel a part of it. He felt brave again. He sang a little, and the Indian smiled down at the strange, young boy in silent approval.

Slowly, slowly the hours moved onward. The dugout moved onward. Everything seemed to be in the midst of an eternity.

Then suddenly, without warning, the day was over. There was no twilight. There was no evening dusk. It was day and then it was night. The sides of the river became canyon walls of blackness, the river rocks were peaks of blackness. It was not a friendly, velvet blackness; it was menacing, terrifying, strange. Beneath the slender dugout the black river roared and thundered.

At last Red saw a light among the trees. It was the Indian encampment. They had almost reached the place.

The dugouts glided to a stop. Dark shapes came down to meet them. Red crawled stiffly from the dugout. He staggered after Lin. He hung his hammock under an open shelter. He wrapped himself in the hammock folds. He fixed his mosquito net tightly around the hammock sides. He did not know where the others were, if they were near him or if they had come at all. He did not care. He slept.

When he awoke at dawn he saw an immense, hilly clearing. The hills around were smooth and rounded and covered with velvet green. Brush shelters like the one he was in dotted a circle where his companions and perhaps a dozen others were sleeping.

Lin gestured to him to wake the others of their party. When they had gathered around him the old Chinese showed them how to fold their nets and hammocks and tie them on their backs. Then they followed him single-file along the river bank, munching the K-rations that Dad had insisted they take with them. They trudged along, too sleepy to be excited, too awed to wake themselves with chatter.

Rounded hill led to higher rounded hill, up and up and up like a broad giant stairway leading skyward. Red was out of breath. He was panting and wet with clammy perspiration. No one else stopped. No one else rested. He wiped the sweat that stung his eyes and blurred his sight as he climbed upward.

On the top of the highest hill Lin stopped them with a single gesture. Red knew without being told that this was the place.

At first he dared not look around. He held his breath, trying to stop his noisy heartbeats. Then Hasteen spoke beside him. He also was breathless. "There is the Bird Woman," he whispered.

Red looked. At the hill's peak was an open shelter, and before it, standing quietly, waiting for them, was the Bird Woman. She was old, old, old. She was the oldest person Red had ever seen. But she was not bent or withered-looking or helpless. She was strong. She stood before them like some magnificent old tree, monarch of all the forest. Old and gnarled, but straight and strong! She had majesty and power. Red felt it and trembled before its strength, but he felt no fear. The Old One's gentle, he thought. She is gentle as God is gentle. Slowly he went forward to meet her.

The Bird Woman spoke to Lin. "She says," the Chinese translated, "to tell you that she knew you were coming. She says to tell the Flaming One that the yellow summer birds have told her."

The old woman spoke again to Lin, and again he translated what she had said. "She says to tell Yellow-Shirt's grandson not to break the pattern of the old, but to strengthen it with wisdom of the world." Lin turned to Juanito, and for the first time since the boys had known him his voice broke with emotion. "She says," Lin told them, "to tell the gentle Juanito welcome. She says to tell him—" The old Chinese could not go on.

Quaco took up the translation. "She says to tell him that though race and color differ, Lin, the old yellow one, loves him as a son."

Red looked at Quaco in surprise. He, too, has many languages, he thought. He smiled at his friend Juanito. "I could have told you," he whispered, "that old Lin loves you as his son."

The Bird Woman motioned them to sit beside her. Gradually the world around them lighted with the sun's first rays. As the sun lighted the clearing the stillness became almost unbearable. Then softly, softly muted twittering sounded among the tree leaves like a wind's whispered song. It was the birds. The birds were coming. Red's heart stood still. His breath stopped in his throat.

Bird calls and bird songs grew louder, louder, louder, accompanied by the whir of wings. The sun burst through the treetops and with its brilliance came the birds.

At first they were just movement—a dipping, darting, skimming, soaring movement. Then the movement took on color—red breasts, red wings, red tail feathers, flashes of yellows and greens and iridescent blues. Then the colors took shape and became birds of all sizes, all shapes, big, small, round, slender.

Little by little Red began to recognize the bird groupings —the twittering swallows, the spinning redwings, the white-rumped sandpipers, the swifts, the many-colored orioles. Little by little the boy began to group the call notes and the songs—the long, sweet song of the wren; the jumbled, warbled song of the oven bird; the sad, lonely call of the killdeer; the unisoned cooing of the turtle doves.

The boys sat spellbound, speechless, without thoughts, without feeling, without a sense of time. The Bird Woman sat beside them, as ancient, as mysterious as the birds she watched.

Lin spoke softly. "Sit here for this day. It will last your lifetime."

Red looked at the old Chinese. This was not the cook in his mother's kitchen. This was a sage of bygone times. He looked at Quaco and Juanito and saw them not as young man and boy, but as men rich with dignity. Slowly his gaze turned to Hasteen. As he expected, he saw a Navajo medicine man binding the wounds of an ancient people.

Juanito broke the silence. "Look at us," he said in wonder. "We represent our races, the races of mankind. We understand one another. We are friends."

The boys looked at one another in wonder and delight.

"We are sharing something that is not given all to share," Hasteen said softly.

Red looked at the thousands of song birds. They know no lands, he thought. They know no boundaries. They sing their songs for the world to hear.

He looked at Hasteen. He said, "This is the end of the long journey."

Hasteen shook his head. "You are wrong, my friend," he answered. "This is the beginning."

Child. Lit. PZ 7 .C5296 Wo 1

Clark, Ann Nolan, 1898-

World song

F

DELTA COLLEGE LIBRARY

CHILD LITERATURE COLLECTION